CROSSFIRE

— Jo Donato —

Crossfire © Jo Donato 2020

Second edition

ISBN: 978-1-922460-27-1 (paperback)

Cover photo by Melodi2 at Morguefile.com.

Published in Australia by Jo Donato and InHouse Publishing.
www.inhousepublishing.com.au

Printed in Australia by InHouse Print & Design.

A catalogue record for this book is available from the National Library of Australia

Acknowledgments

Special thanks to my husband for all your patience and support, and to my two darling children, Ethan and Maya, for letting me sit quietly in my writing room to work on my novel.

Chapter 1

As I stood in front of my full-length mirror examining the finished product, I glanced around my bedroom. Nothing had changed since I was a small child. The walls were still painted soft pink; I still had my shaggy brown carpet and my double-storey Victorian doll's house stood in the corner collecting dust.

I looked back at my reflection and sighed.

You look beautiful, Harper.

That's another thing that hadn't changed: I was still hearing the male voice in my head.

"Hmm, I guess I polished up okay," I told myself as I turned to the left to look at the dress my nanna had made me.

You look more than okay, the voice said.

I smiled to myself.

It was a beautiful cream-coloured silk-satin and lace ensemble. I gingerly ran my fingers over the lace neckline. Turning to my right, I truly saw the beauty of the dress, which was trimmed with lace and faux pearl decorations across the bodice and hem. I continued running my fingers lightly over the shirred, slightly dropped waist.

I marvelled at the detail of the small floral decoration at my hip, with its thin streamers trailing down to the hemline.

Words could not explain how truly beautiful the dress was. I wanted to look extra special tonight; I didn't wear dresses… ever, but tonight was a special night.

I slipped on my strappy heels and draped a shawl across my shoulders just as the doorbell rang.

"I'll get it," I called to my parents, who were in the living room down the corridor.

Our house has two storeys with three bedrooms, the bathroom, kitchen and living room all upstairs. Downstairs, well that's what sets our house apart from everyone else's.

You see, we share our house with dead people. Charming, I know. My father owns a funeral business right here in the family casa. That's right, I come home some days to find a closed casket in the middle of the front foyer.

Don't get me wrong; it's okay when you have grown up walking into the house to find a coffin smack bang in the middle of the room, but new friends didn't stay friends for long, if you know what I mean. It freaks them out.

Making my way downstairs, I tried not to fall; heels and I were not a good mix. Tonight there was no coffin in the foyer, only a round mahogany table with a stunning arrangement of red and black Fox Dahlias arranged in a stylish frosted vase.

Opening the front door, I was greeted by a crisp, cool night air and Ryan, my handsome date, standing there looking his finest in a black suit, white shirt and black tie.

"Wow, Harper, you look amazing!"

I turned a full circle for him in my new dress.

"Thanks, you didn't scrub up too bad yourself," I smiled.

"Is that Ryan?" Mother called from the top of the staircase. "Wait, wait, just one photo before you leave," she said, racing down the stairs in her flannelette pyjamas and fluffy slippers. Her ebony hair was tied loosely in a ponytail and her green eyes were sparkling. Even in that state she looked truly beautiful.

I was lucky enough to have inherited my mother's eye colour.

"Mother, really?" I could feel my cheeks turning red.

"Oh come on, Harper, it's only one photo." Ryan smiled, placing his arm around me.

Ryan would do anything for my mother; I guess she was the mother he never had. In a flash of blinding light, she took the photo.

"You two look just gorgeous." She smiled, pulling a tissue out of her sleeve.

"Mother, no tears, you promised," I said, giving her a warning look.

"Sorry." She smiled, wiping away a single tear with the back of her hand. "Have fun and drive carefully," she said, ushering us out the door and heading back inside before her tears started flowing non-stop.

"You do look truly amazing tonight, Harper," Ryan said, as his eyes wandered over me.

For the first time in my fourteen years of knowing Ryan, he had made me blush!

"Thank you. I guess it's a change from my usual jeans and Converse sneakers," I replied.

"Sure is. Shall we get going to the dance?" Ryan asked as he held out his hand for me to take.

I took it in mine as he escorted me over to his black 1966 hardtop Mustang. He opened the passenger door for me, and I got in. I glanced across the road to the forest that runs the whole length of the street, and in the fog, something caught my eye.

I could just make out a tall figure by the tree. He was dressed completely in black, from the hooded jumper that covered his head and most of his face right down to his jeans and sneakers.

"Are you okay?" Ryan asked as he got in and closed the door.

"Do you see him?" I asked, my breath fogging the glass.

Ryan leant forward to look past me. "Him who?"

I turned to him, dumbfounded. "You didn't see him?" I asked, pointing back over my shoulder.

By the time I had turned back around, the figure was gone.

"That's odd," I said, leaning closer to the window. I could have sworn I'd seen some black feathers floating to the ground.

"What is?" Ryan asked, starting the car.

"Doesn't matter." I frowned, sitting back in my seat.

"You're not seeing things again, are you?" he questioned.

"Again?" I asked, looking over at him.

"Yeah, remember when we were ten? You swore that you could see a man all in black out in your garden."

"No." I lied, not wanting to relive the memory.

"Yeah, and it got even creepier when we were fifteen and you said that you would see him standing at the end of your bed nearly every night."

"I did?"

"Yes. Why do you think we always had sleepovers at my place? I think maybe you got the spooks growing up in that house." He smiled.

I looked back out the window. "Hmm, maybe."

"I guess two years of therapy made you forget, huh?" Ryan added.

"Yeah, I guess." I nodded.

Until tonight.

As Ryan pulled the car onto the road, I looked out at the forest of dark trees rushing by. I figured Ryan was right: two years of therapy had made me forget all about the mysterious figure that has haunted my life since I was little. The therapy may have made me not see him, but I still heard him loud and clear.

I settled back in my seat and thought back to when Ryan and I first met. We were both three years old when he moved in next door with his father after his mother died suddenly. Since we were both only children, my parents and Ryan's father thought it would be a wonderful idea for us to become playmates. So that was that. We spent every waking hour together, and our parents made sure we were always in the same class right to this very day.

Ryan reached for my hand and gently squeezed it, bringing me back to the present.

"You okay?" he asked, glancing my way.

"Yeah, why?"

"You seem a little distant," he said, facing the road again.

"I'm okay," I lied again; it was becoming a habit tonight.

"You sure?" He looked at me.

I nodded my head.

A soft mist had rolled in and the slight drizzle falling from the dark night sky was enough for Ryan to switch on the windscreen wipers. I watched them as they pushed the rain away.

"Okay, no more questions," he said and smiled, focusing his attention back onto the wet road in front of us.

School wasn't close to us. It took us almost twenty-five minutes to drive there.

"Say, Ryan, can I ask you something?"

"Anything, Harper, you know you don't have to ask first."

"Well, it's just that—" I paused for a moment, trying to get my words right.

"What is it, H? The suspense is killing me." He looked over at me.

I let out a nervous sigh. "How come you've never asked me to be your girlfriend?" My words came out rushed, and I could feel my cheeks turning crimson red. Thank God it was dark in the car.

"What? Harper I never, I mean it's like, well, I guess I never thought of you that way."

"Oh?" I turned in my chair to face him.

"Hold on." Ryan pulled the car off the road, turned to face me and took my hand in his. "I guess I never really wanted to ruin our friendship. I love what you and I have, I can trust you, tell you anything, and most of all, you never judge me."

I gave him a small smile. "Okay."

"I have wanted to, you know?"

"Wanted to?" I asked.

"Yeah, to ask you to be my girlfriend."

"Really?" I blushed.

Ryan moved as close to me as possible and placed his cold hand on my flushed cheek. Without a word, and to my surprise, he leant towards me, slowly parting his lips. This was it, the moment I had been waiting for. His smell of aftershave was intoxicating.

Without hesitation, I moved closer to him, our lips almost touching, when suddenly a massive crack of thunder roared overhead, causing us to both jump back in our seats.

"Whoa! That was a big one." Ryan laughed uneasily as he looked out his window.

As I glanced out the front windscreen, lightning illuminated the sky, and I saw a figure standing a couple of feet in front of the car.

"Ryan, look!"

But the darkness had returned.

"What am I looking at, Harper? I don't see anything,"

"Nothing. It's okay, let's just go."

"What about our kiss?" he asked playfully, giving me a cheeky smile.

"Maybe later?"

Ryan nodded. "Okay," he said, pulling the car back onto the road.

"I'm sorry, Ryan, I just want to get to the dance."

"You don't need to apologize, Harper, it's okay."

"Thank you."

The rain began to fall faster, heavier, making the road difficult to see clearly.

"This rain is crazy." An uneasy laugh escaped Ryan's lips.

"Are you okay to drive? Do you need to pull over?"

"No, I think you're right, it's best to get to the dance."

I nodded my head, not saying anything, just letting Ryan concentrate on the road ahead.

Suddenly, something shot out from the forest and stopped dead in the middle of the road.

"What in God's name?" Ryan yelled.

He hit the brakes hard and turned the steering wheel sharply to the right, trying to avoid what was standing in the middle of the road. The tires slipped and the car spun out of control before straightening up again.

"Ryan, watch out!" I shouted, as I gripped onto the dashboard.

"SHIT!" he yelled, pumping his foot on and off the brake.

It was useless. The brakes had failed.

"RYAN!" I screamed, as he lost total control of the car, sending it down the steep embankment.

He frantically pumped the brakes. "The brakes aren't working," he yelled, causing me to jump.

As the dark forest trees whooshed by us at an alarming speed and rain continued to fall, Ryan held desperately to the steering wheel, turning it frantically as he attempted to avoid hitting the trees. How he managed to miss every single one of them as we careened down the steep hill was beyond me.

"We're going to die!" I screamed at him.

"Sit back in your seat, don't lean forward, just stay calm."

I could hear panic rising in his voice.

"Stay calm? How do you suppose I do that?" I screamed at him, as the forest trees seemed to close in on us.

It's going to be over soon, the voice whispered.

But something was wrong. The voice was different to the voice I had always heard before.

Before Ryan could say anything, the car became airborne, flipped in mid-air, then came down hard on its roof, skidding to a stop inches from a bough of a fallen tree.

I could feel something warm trickling down the side of my face. I rolled my head to look at Ryan. He was slumped in his seat, his eyes closed.

Blood covered his face in the most horrifying way. I felt my stomach turning, I felt like I was going to throw up.

"Ryan?" I barely whispered, as my teeth chattered uncontrollably. I couldn't stop my body from shaking.

There was no answer from him, no movement; just an eerie silence.

"Ryan, please, please?" I begged.

I couldn't move, I was pinned against the dashboard. The taste of warm blood in my mouth was making me nauseous.

I closed my eyes for a moment, not believing what just happened, that any of this was real.

"Help! Somebody help us!" I cried out. But there was no one to hear my screams.

There was still no movement from Ryan. "Please, please, Ryan, wake up." It pained me to look at him.

Suddenly I heard a crunching sound outside my smashed window. It sounded like twigs and glass was being stepped on.

I rolled my aching head to look outside. The headlights shone onto a tree, causing the dimming lights to bounce back my way.

A figure all in black stood by my side of the car. I couldn't see their face; they were too tall.

"Help us," I gasped. "Please."

The silence made my ears ring.

Without a word, he let a black feather fall from his fingertips. It fell like a fresh snowflake falling from the sky. It drifted down to the ground, finding its resting place next to his black motorcycle boot. He shifted his foot slightly as if annoyed by the feather's presence.

I felt my eyelids getting heavier and heavier until I could no longer keep them open.

Chapter 2

I woke from my sleep startled and disorientated, a tube in my nose and a machine beeping irritably beside me. I watched as a doctor in a white coat checked a clipboard at the foot of my bed.

He raised his eyes to me.

"Ah, Miss O'Connor, I see you are finally fully awake."

Finally? Fully awake? What did he mean by that?

I tried to sit up a little but found I was being held captive by a mass of tiny wires strapped to my body and an IV needle sticking out the back of my hand.

"Where am I?" I croaked. My throat was dry.

The smell of disinfectant and bleach was overpowering and making me feel sick.

"Paradise Community Hospital," he said and smiled as he picked up my wrist to check my pulse.

I looked over his perfect features. His skin was flawless, and his teeth perfectly straight and white. How could someone be that beautiful?

I could feel my cheeks turning a little red.

"I'll call your mother in." He gave me a small wink as he flashed me a smile, heading out of the room.

"Harper?" Mother called stepping through the doorway.

Relief washed over me as she crossed over the room and walked quickly over to my bed. She hugged me as best she could.

"Oh sweetie, this time we thought we had lost you."

"What are you talking about? Why am I here hooked up to all these machines?" I honestly had no idea what I was doing lying in a hospital bed.

She pulled up a chair, sat down and reached for my non-needle hand.

"You were in an accident, honey, and you have been in the hospital all week. Your father and I have been so worried."

We sat there in silence, Mother with her thoughts and me with mine. Then suddenly it hit me, and memories flooded back to me as if it had happened yesterday.

A single tear rolled down my flushed cheek. "Ryan? Where's Ryan?" I panicked, and the ECG machine picked up my quickening heartbeat.

"Harper, you have to take a deep breath and stay calm," she said soothingly.

"Stay calm," I repeated as I recalled Ryan's final words to me.

"Do you need me to get the doctor?" she asked.

He's gone, Harper. The voice whispered. It was the usual voice I heard.

I shook my head as more tears escaped my eyes. "He's dead… isn't he?" I swallowed, trying to get past the lump in my throat.

"Oh Harper, I'm sorry love, there was nothing the doctors could do. By the time they reached Ryan, well he died on impact, Harper, I'm sorry."

"They?"

"Yes." She frowned. "The people that were driving behind you when…"

The doctor had re-entered the room. "When Ryan ran the car off the road." He finished her sentence.

I glared at him. How dare he?

"Honey do you remember what happened, anything at all?" Mother continued.

It pained me to say Ryan's name, to relive the nightmare. I swallowed before I started reliving the horror.

"Ryan and I were driving to the school dance. It was raining and a low mist had rolled in. Suddenly something from the forest ran out in front of the car and stopped dead in the middle of the road. Ryan spun the wheel trying to avoid hitting it. That's when he lost control, that's when we careered off the road down the embankment." I glared at the doctor. "He did not run the car off the road." I sneered. "You make it sound like he did it on purpose."

"No, dear," Mother said quickly. "That's not what the doctor was saying, we are just trying to work out what happened, that's all. Right, doctor?" She turned to him.

He hadn't taken his eyes from mine. "Must have been a racoon," Doctor Creepy commented.

"It was much bigger than a racoon," I sniped, as I looked over him and his good looks.

"Deer, perhaps?" He smirked, raising an eyebrow.

He was watching me intently, not blinking, not taking his eyes from mine.

I broke the gaze and turned to my mother. "When can I go home? I don't want to be here anymore."

"Well, Harper, that is up to Doctor Raphael."

I turned to look at the doctor, who was still staring at me. I shook my head. "Well?" I prompted. "Can I go home?"

He looked down at his clipboard, then back up to me, and then over to my mother. "I have some notes here from Mr O'Connor that the funeral is tomorrow, is that correct?"

She looked at me hesitantly, then back to the doctor. "Yes, that is correct."

"And I take it your husband is conducting the funeral?"

Like duh, we were the only funeral parlour in town. What a stupid question to ask.

"Of course," she answered, sounding thrown off by his odd question.

"Then I'd like to keep Harper here for the night. You can pick her up in the morning."

"What? No! I feel fine." I protested. "Mother, please? Don't leave me here another night. I want to go home," I begged, looking from her to the doctor.

Doctor Creepy flashed me a smile. "Harper, dear, how you walked away from that accident with a mild concussion and a few scratches is beyond me."

A cold chill ran down my spine, making me shiver. There was something odd about him I just couldn't put my finger on.

"Well it's not the first time," Mother added, a little embarrassed.

The doctor looked down at the clipboard and flicked through the pages. "Yes, I see she is a regular at this hospital," he said, running his finger down the page.

"Admitted when she was three, almost drowned in the lake, but managed to survive. Hit by a car while riding her bike at the age of ten, survived that with only a broken leg. At fourteen, skateboarded through a shop window, survived with only a few scratches and a broken wrist. Now a car accident at seventeen and you survived that with a few cuts and bruises and a mild concussion. My, my, Harper, if I may say so, you must have one powerful angel watching over your shoulder, or is it the devil is trying to kill you?" He laughed.

Why was he the only one laughing? What a bizarre thing to say, and why did he say "survived" at the end of every accident?

"Yes, well she is and always has been an accident-prone child." Mother laughed, standing up to leave.

"You're going?" I panicked. I didn't want to spend another minute in this place with Doctor Looney.

"Yes, sweetie, the doctor thinks it's best for you to stay another night. You have a big day ahead of you tomorrow," she said as she kissed the top of my head.

"Fine," I huffed. "I guess I'll see you in the morning," I said, disappointed.

"I'll pick you up, so you'll have time to go home and have a shower before…" She paused.

"It's okay, Mother, I get it. Bye," I said, sighing.

She nodded as she went over to the door and stopped next to Doctor Raphael.

"Be sure she eats something, and I want to know if she starts talking to herself again," she whispered, although not so softly that I couldn't hear her.

He nodded his head and waited for Mother to leave before he made his way back over to my bed.

"So, Harper," he began, sitting down in the chair. "Tell me about these voices your mother was just talking about."

She didn't say voices, she said I talk to myself.

"I don't hear voices," I lied.

"No? Are you sure? It's okay if you do, Harper. We all have our own special talents."

"If I did hear voices, I wouldn't discuss them with you."

"No? Why not?" he asked, his creepy little smile making its way out again.

"Because I don't like you."

"Well you should like me, Harper, I am one of many who saved your life," he said, his green eyes flashing.

I watched him carefully as he ran his hand through his sandy blond hair; this guy would put Greek Gods to shame!

"I want you to leave now," I told him firmly.

"I'd like to know more about these voices you hear," he said as he leant back in the chair.

"You're not going to give up, are you?" I asked.

He shook his head. "I am your doctor, after all." He smirked.

"Fine."

"Good." He folded his arms across his chest and watched me closely.

"When I was three, after I almost drowned, I started hearing a voice in my head."

"Was it a male or a female voice?"

What an odd question. "Male. Anyway, I often talked to him. I never saw anyone, just heard the voice. One day my mother caught me talking to the wall in my room and took me to see a shrink. As I got older, from time to time I would see a boy, like a teenage boy all in black, sometimes in the garden or at the foot of my bed."

I watched Doctor Raphael close his eyes.

"Are you okay?" I asked.

He opened them again. "Go on."

"He went away for a while until…" my voice drifted off.

Doctor Raphael leant forward closer to the bed. "Until?"

"Until the night of the accident." I closed my eyes.

"You saw him the night of the accident?" He pushed.

"No. I heard him." I didn't open my eyes. I was through talking.

I heard the chair being pushed back on the linoleum floor. I kept my eyes shut.

"Get some rest, Harper, I'll organize a nurse to bring you dinner."

His voice sounded low, troubled even. I nodded my head and waited for him to leave the room and close the door before I opened my eyes again.

It was quiet in the sterile room except for the beeping of my machine and the sound of two angry male voices arguing on the other side of my door. I strained my ears to hear what was being said.

"What were you thinking, interfering like that?" Doctor Raphael spat.

"I'm sorry."

"You're sorry? You are messing with things, you know that?"

"I know, Raphael, I've fallen."

"You can stop, walk away. She is old enough now. You know what will happen to you, right?" the doctor asked.

"Yes, Raphael, I am willing for that to happen to me for her."

"And give up everything?" Doctor Raphael sighed.

"Yes."

"All for a girl?"

"Yes."

"And him?" the doctor questioned.

"I won't let him win."

"She won't understand. It will be too much for her to comprehend."

There was a pause. Who was Doctor Raphael talking to? Why wasn't the other person addressing him as 'doctor'?

"Then help me, Raphael, please?"

"I can't." There was a pause. "She's not the only one, you know that?"

"I know, but I don't want him to do this, not to her or others."

A shiver ran down my spine. What on heaven's earth were they talking about? Who were they talking about?

"You are being stubborn, childish. I suggest you grow up!"

I quickly lay back down and closed my eyes when I heard the door handle click. The door opened, then shut again. I opened my eyes and let out a big sigh. That conversation was intense. I wondered who and what they were talking about.

The door opened again, and a nurse carrying a tray walked across the room towards me.

"Well, Miss O'Connor, it's good to see you awake and with some colour in your cheeks. Let me remove all these wires. You don't need them anymore."

I watched as the nurse busied herself.

"Um, nurse?"

"Yes dear?"

"Who was Doctor Raphael talking to just now?"

She stopped pressing buttons on the machine and looked over at the door then back to me. "Nobody." She shrugged.

"But I..."

"I said nobody," she hissed, giving me a warning look.

"Oh, I'm sorry." I said, sinking back into my pillows.

Geez, what was her problem?

"Have your dinner, miss, then get some sleep."

I nodded my head at her as she turned and left the room. Lifting the heavy silver lid off the main plate, I looked down at what was for dinner.

"Mmm, mashed vegetables hidden by cold gravy and is that chicken?" I said as I moved the soggy peas around the plate.

"Is there a problem, Harper?"

I looked up, startled. "Doctor Raphael, I didn't hear you come in."

He crossed over the room and stopped at the end of the bed.

"You're not hungry?" he asked.

I placed the fork down and looked up at him. His green eyes met mine.

"I guess I've lost my appetite all of a sudden."

"You really don't like me, do you?" He smirked.

Seriously?

"There's something I don't like about you," I replied honestly.

"Okay," he answered.

Okay? Was that it? No more to be said?

"It's okay, Harper, you don't have to like me. No one is forcing you to," he said as he picked up the folder.

"Doctor Raphael, can I ask you something?"

He looked across the bed at me. "Sure."

"Who were you talking to just outside my door before?" I asked, watching him carefully.

He shrugged. "Nobody."

"Nobody? Don't lie, I heard you arguing with another male just outside my door."

"I don't know what you are talking about, Harper," he said and looked back down at the paper.

I pushed the bed table aside, lay back down on the pillow and closed my eyes.

"See to it you eat, Harper," he said as he walked over to the door.

I watched him exit the room and close the door behind him. All of a sudden, I felt extremely tired and couldn't keep my eyes open.

I closed my heavy eyelids, and then opened them again. When I looked across the room, I saw a figure dressed all in black, standing in the corner of the room, facing me.

"Doctor Raphael?" I slurred, overcome by tiredness.

Why was I so tired all of a sudden? The room was warm, too warm, and I so desperately wanted to sleep.

The dark figure shook his head. "Sleep now," he whispered, his voice floating across the room towards me.

I smiled sheepishly as his velvety words danced slowly through my mind.

"Who are you?" I slurred.

I could hardly keep my eyes open.

"Sleep now," he said again.

I gave in, closed my heavy eyelids and fell into a dreamless sleep.

Chapter 3

When I woke the following morning, it must have still been dark outside. Sunshine hadn't found its way into the room and for a moment I thought I was home, safe and warm in my bed, until I focused on the dull light coming from the beige lamp on my bedside table.

The overpowering smell of disinfectant and bleach brought me back to reality—hospital—I was still there.

So it was real, all of it. I looked at the back of my right hand. Tiny crisscross cuts were slowly starting to heal. I was alive, and Ryan wasn't. Somehow, I managed to survive the accident that took my best friend, my only friend, away from me.

But how was that possible? What did Doctor Creepy say? I've either got a guardian angel watching me or the devil trying to kill me. I shuddered at the thought.

Suddenly flashes of that night danced in my head like a movie in slow motion. I blinked hard at the pictures moving through my mind; piece by piece, it all came together.

The car flipped, became airborne and came down hard on its roof. It was as if some great force pushed us off the road. I closed my eyes and tried to remember.

And then I saw him.

The mysterious figure dressed all in black that came out of nowhere and stood in the middle of the road. He raised his left hand before moving it across his chest at lightning speed. That was the last I saw of him before the car went off the road.

I sat up quickly; my heart beat hard against my chest, making it difficult for me to breathe.

"Good morning, Miss O'Connor, did you sleep well?"

I looked over at the nurse, who was watching me as she opened the curtains.

Had she been there the whole time?

I pretended to yawn. "What time is it?"

"Five thirty, miss, your parents will be here soon."

I glanced around the room then down to my hand. A tiny round Band-Aid had replaced the needle in the back of my hand.

"Am I going home?"

"Yes, miss, as soon as you have had something to eat." She smiled as she left the room.

Why did all the nurses keep calling me "miss"? What an unusual way to address someone.

I shook my head as I threw back the white waffle-weave blanket and sheet. Slowly I lowered my feet down onto the cold, dull-grey linoleum floor.

"Going somewhere, Harper?"

Startled, I looked up to find Doctor Raphael standing in the room with my breakfast tray.

"Yeah, home." I was in no mood to talk to him at five thirty in the morning.

"Not until you have breakfast first." He smiled as he made his way over to the bed and placed the tray down.

I watched him carefully as he stepped away from the bed.

For some reason I felt uncomfortable around him. His good looks unnerved me. He looked too young to be a doctor.

"You're staring at me." He smiled. "And you seem to be blushing," he teased.

I shook my head at him and chose to ignore his comment as I pulled my feet back up and tucked them under the blanket.

"Are you going to eat?" he asked.

"Hmm let me see," I began, looking over the contents on the tray. "Cold toast served with frozen butter, a tea bag dunked once in warm tap water, and what's this?" I lifted the lid off the plate. "Mush with raisins to make it look more appealing. No thanks," I said as I covered the puke-like substance with the heavy lid.

"Are you always this happy in the morning, Harper?" he asked as he folded his arms across his chest.

I gave him a blank look, watching him. "Should I be happy? My best friend is dead, I don't know how or why I survived that accident, and to top it off, I'm stuck here in this hellhole talking to you. I don't know why you are keeping me in here like a prisoner for so long if I only had a mild concussion. You'd be anything but happy, I'm sure," I snapped.

"Eat your breakfast and then get dressed. Your parents will be here soon," he said as he walked out the room.

"Eat your breakfast," I mimicked him as the door slowly closed behind him.

I looked down over the tray of uninviting food, then pushed it aside. Who was he to tell me what to do? I got out of bed and found my jeans, long-sleeved top and Converse sneakers piled neatly on a green chair.

As I stood on the cold floor staring at my clothes, a shiver ran down my back. I quickly got dressed and tied my shoelaces in a single knot.

"It's going to be okay, Harper."

"What?" I spun around. "Who said that?"

There was no response. I was alone in the room.

"Harper?"

I turned to the door and watched as it slowly opened. It was my parents. I was so relieved to see them. I raced over to them and hugged them.

"It's good to see you, honey, I'm sorry I haven't visited often lately it's just that..."

I looked up at my father as he glanced over at my mother, who gave him a little nod. He pulled away from me and looked into my eyes.

"It's okay, Dad, you don't need to explain anything." I comforted him as a tear rolled down his pale cheek.

He shook his head as if lost for words.

"I never… not Ryan… I'm sorry, Harper," he said as he wiped the tear away.

"Don't cry, Dad, everything is going to be all right." I was trying to convince myself as much as him.

He let out a big sigh and nodded his head. "Let's go home."

He placed his arm around my shoulders and walked me out of the room. We slowly strolled down the corridor, side by side. Neither one of us were in a hurry to get back home. As we walked into the waiting room, Doctor Raphael came around the corner.

"Ah, Harper, I was just coming to see if you were all set to go home?" He smiled.

I looked up into his eyes. Either I was seeing things, or his eyes were darker than they had been this morning. I was sure they had been lighter earlier.

"Harper?" Mother interrupted my thoughts.

I pulled my head straight. "What?"

"Doctor Raphael asked you a question, honey," Dad said as he looked from my mother to me. "It's rude not to answer."

I bit my bottom lip. Doctor Raphael's eyes never left mine. "Yes," I said, although I wasn't sure if he had asked a question or not.

"Well then, you take care now, Harper, I don't want to see you in here anytime soon," he said and smiled at me.

I nodded my head and followed my parents outside.

"A taxi?" I asked, disappointed.

"Yes well, the family car is needed for today sweetie." Dad hesitated.

"Oh."

Our family car was no ordinary family car; it was a hearse. It wasn't a modern-day hearse either; not a Mercedes or a Ford. It was a restored 1956 black Cadillac hearse.

I loved that hearse. Winged taillights, thick lace curtains covering the side windows, white wall tires and front grille snarling like it's going to come alive and eat you, that kind of hearse.

I let out a big sigh before we all climbed into the taxi. Dad rode in the front with the driver and I sat in the back with my mother, who was watching me a little too carefully.

I looked out the window and up to the second floor of the hospital and saw Doctor Raphael staring down at me from behind the glass. I could see his lips moving. He was talking to someone who was standing next to him, someone who was dressed all in black.

A cold chill ran down my spine as the taxi pulled away.

It was quiet in the taxi. The only words spoken were Dad's directions to the taxi driver, which were directions to our house, the O'Connor Family Funeral Parlour.

Although the drive home wasn't long, the walk up the six front steps to the porch seemed to take forever. I took the key out of my mother's hand.

"Are you sure you don't want to use the back door?" she offered.

Ignoring her, I reached for the door handle and placed the key in the lock. Dad put his hand on my shoulder, and I turned around to face him.

"Harper, I just want you to know…"

"I already know, Dad. I know what's waiting behind this door. It is no different to other days I have come home."

"Harper sweetie, all we are trying to say is …"

"I get it, Mother, I'm okay," I lied.

I turned the silver knob and pushed the door open.

And there it was. Ryan's coffin.

Ryan's dad had chosen a pristine white coffin with silver hardware. It was beautiful.

It didn't seem real. I touched the top of the coffin and ran my hand along the smooth, cold surface.

"I want to see him," I told my dad, my voice wavering.

It was a bold request to make. He always respected the wishes of the deceased's family; he took his job very seriously. Today I didn't care. Not this time, not with Ryan lying underneath that lid.

"Mr Wood has requested a closed casket for today's service, honey," he explained in his best funeral director's voice.

I shot my father a look; I couldn't care less what Ryan's father had requested.

"It won't hurt, Phil. It would probably be good for Harper to see him one last time, to say her goodbyes with no one else here," my mother said as she turned to my dad.

He nodded his head and slowly lifted the lid. "Do you want us to stay?" he asked.

I shook my head no.

I waited for them to leave the room before I took in a deep breath and looked in the coffin. Ryan looked different, peaceful. I closed my eyes and kissed Ryan's ice-cold pale lips. I opened my eyes and pulled back.

"Our first kiss. I miss you so much already," I told him as I placed my hand over his.

Tears fell from my eyes into the coffin. I desperately tried to wipe them away. "I don't know what happened, but I know you saw him this time," I whispered.

I ran my fingers over a raised scar that ran down the side of his face. It hadn't been there before the accident. "You look so beautiful," I whispered sadly.

"It's going to be okay, Harper, I promise." A male voice spoke softly from a darkened corner of the front foyer.

"Who are you? I, I can't see you."

"Harper? Are you okay, sweetie?" Mother called from the other room.

Suddenly I became very cold and I began to shake.

"I'm fine," I said, unable to stop my teeth from chattering.

Why was it so damn cold in here all of a sudden?

"Do you want me to come in there?" she asked.

"No, I'm okay," I lied.

I turned back and looked down at Ryan.

"I'm going to miss you. You were my only friend. Now I have nobody." I began to weep uncontrollably.

"Harper?"

I looked up to find mother standing on the other side of the coffin. I'm glad she didn't ask me any more questions. She just gave me a sympathetic look.

"It's time, sweetie. You have to go get ready."

I nodded my head and looked back down at Ryan.

"Goodbye, Ryan, I'll miss you and just so you know, I did love you."

Just as I finished speaking, the lights overhead flickered. Mother and I both looked up.

"Oh dear, I hope we don't have a blackout," she said, looking back down at me.

It suddenly became icy again and I began to shiver.

"Sweetie, if you need to talk..." she began as she closed the lid on the coffin.

I watched as it lowered slowly. "I'm fine, I just want this day to be over with," I replied and turned to leave.

Reality set in as I made my way upstairs to my room. I closed the door behind me and started to cry again.

A photo on my dresser of me and Ryan caught my eye. It was taken on our first day at school, when we were five years old. We were holding hands and our smiles matched our oversized backpacks.

"Why Ryan? Why not me too?" I sobbed.

"Harper? Are you okay?" Dad called from behind the closed door.

I wiped my eyes, pulled myself together and opened the door.

"I'm fine, Dad, thanks," I said, giving him a weak smile.

He smiled hesitantly. "Okay, well you have about half an hour before the service starts."

"Sure. I'll be ready."

I went into the bathroom, closed the door and ran the water in the shower, waited for the room to fill up with steam, then got undressed and stepped in. The hot, stinging droplets felt good on my cold skin. The shower was comforting and calming, and I didn't want to leave it, but I knew time was ticking and the front foyer would be getting quite full.

As I stepped out of the bathroom, I could hear my mother talking to a lady downstairs.

"So, how is Harper doing? It must be tough on her to lose her one and only friend."

"She's holding up okay," Mother replied.

Stupid small-town folk with their nosey gossip. I shook my head as I made my way back to my room.

I slammed the door hard, dried off and got dressed. I tied my hair in a ponytail, applied some black eyeliner and mascara, and stepped out into the corridor.

"Oh, Harper, honey, I thought you were already downstairs," dad said, startled.

"Nope, going now."

"Dressed like that?" he asked, shocked.

I looked down at my tight black jeans, black lace-up combat boots and my black long-sleeved top and then back up to my father.

"Yeah?"

I didn't see a problem; this was how I always dressed when I was with Ryan.

"But Harper, I thought you would put on something a bit more appropriate for the funeral."

"I am who I am, Dad, I'm not faking an appearance for a bunch of people I don't know!" I snapped as I walked away from him.

As I headed downstairs feeling numb, I noticed the foyer was quite full; some people I knew, but most I didn't.

I saw my mother watching me from across the room. Her eyes never left me for a second.

"Harper?"

I turned around. "Mr Wood?"

"I'm sorry, Harper, you two were so close," he said, as a single tear rolled down his cheek.

Before I could say anything, he turned and went to sit down in the front row. I took my seat at the back, trying to avoid people. The room began to fill quite quickly. Who were all these people?

"Harper?" Mother whispered, as she suddenly appeared next to me. "Is there a reason why you are sitting all the way back here?"

"I don't want to sit too close to the front. I'm fine back here. Okay?"

She patted my hand and smiled. "Okay."

As soon as Dad stood at the podium, the room fell quiet. I looked around at the sombre faces. Half of them I'd never seen before.

When Dad finished delivering the beautiful service, Mother turned to me.

"Are you ready to head over to the cemetery? Do you want to grab your coat?"

"I'm ready, and no, I don't want my coat."

We stood up and I followed my mother outside. It was cold, icy cold, and dark storm clouds were rolling in overhead.

The cemetery was just nine houses down the road. That was what you got when you lived in a small town.

"Are you okay to walk?" Mother asked, as we slowly fell behind a group of women dressed in black.

I nodded my head.

We made our way across the freshly mowed lawn and over to a marquee set up for the funeral.

"Our seats are at the front. Mr Wood requested we sit there with him," she told me as she slipped her arm through mine.

This didn't feel real; it felt like my body didn't belong to me and that I was somehow in the middle of a dream.

I looked down at the single white rose that lay on each of the front seats. I picked up one and smelt it.

I sat down in front of the coffin and watched as seats on the other side began to fill up. The priest arrived and everyone stood up. I glanced over the crowd of people and saw a boy around my age standing at the back. He looked familiar but I didn't know why.

He was taller than me and his dark brown hair hung across his left eye. He was watching me. I began to feel cold and started to shake. Mother turned to me.

"Harper? Are you okay, honey? I did ask you to bring your coat," she whispered.

"I'm cold, like really, really cold," I said through clenched teeth.

I couldn't take my eyes off of him; his skin was flawless. I watched as a smile crept across his blood-red lips.

"Harper, it's cold but not that cold. You are shaking pretty badly. Here, take my coat," she murmured softly as she slipped it off her shoulders.

The priest stopped talking and every set of eyes across the coffin looked at me.

It was quiet, so quiet that my ears started to ring.

I didn't know what was happening. Why was he staring at me like that? Who was that boy? And why was he smiling?

This wasn't the time or place for smiles. I turned to look at my mother, who was gaping at me.

"I, I don't feel right." I swallowed.

I could feel the blood draining from my face; everything was going in and out of focus.

"Harper!" Mother yelled.

Her voice seemed to be coming from a long way away.

Then I began to fall.

Everything went pitch black.

Chapter 4

"**D**o you think it is time, Doctor Raphael? It would be best for her, won't it?"

My eyelids fluttered open to the sound of Mother's voice. I sat up fast and looked around frantically. She wasn't in the room. She was standing in the corridor behind the closed door.

I breathed a sigh of relief as I looked around my room at all my things. I was home.

"It is a decision you have to make. You know she will be safe there."

I would be safe where?

"I'm worried about her."

"She will be fine there, Mrs O'Connor. I can assure you this won't happen again."

What wouldn't happen again? What were they talking about?

"Would you like a cuppa before you leave?" she asked, as they headed downstairs.

"Thank you but no, I must be on my way."

I climbed out of bed and caught my reflection in the mirror. I was a mess and wearing my pyjamas at four fifteen in the afternoon.

What the hell was going on?

"Mother?" I called out.

Within seconds, she was racing up the stairs and into my room.

"What is it, Harper, are you okay? Do you feel faint? Why are you out of bed?"

I looked at her suspiciously. "What's with all the questions? Why am I in bed in the first place?" I questioned her.

She took my hand in hers and sat me down on the bed, then sat next to me.

"Harper, you fainted at Ryan's funeral this morning. You hit your head pretty hard on the coffin."

"Oh, that's embarrassing." I blushed.

"I had Doctor Raphael come over to make sure you're okay." She looked at me with worry in her eyes. "Harper, if anything is bothering you or you just want to talk, you know I am here for you, okay?"

"Anything?"

"Yes dear, anything."

"I'm seeing him again," I said in a rush, watching her reaction.

She was still holding my hand. "Who, honey?" She frowned.

"Umm, the shadow man." I bit my bottom lip.

With the look my mother was giving me, I wished I never mentioned it.

"Harper, honey, I thought therapy fixed all that?"

"It did, for a while, a long while but I saw him again the night of the accident."

She laughed a little uneasily. "It was a forest animal, Harper, that was all." She let go of my hand and began picking at the blanket.

"No, Mother that is not all. I heard him; he spoke to me today, when we got home from the hospital, when you and Dad left me alone to be with Ryan."

My mother let out a frustrated sigh. "And what did he say to you, Harper?"

"He told me that it was going to be okay."

"Harper, listen, you were in a very bad accident, you were knocked unconscious, your best friend died. It is a lot to take on board, honey."

"But?" I sulked.

"No, end of discussion. When you were younger, I could tolerate you talking to the walls. It was cute, you had an imaginary friend. But now that you are seventeen, eighteen soon, it has got to stop."

"For God's sake, you tell me to talk to you, and when I do, you tell me off!" I yelled at her.

"Don't you raise your voice at me, young lady," she replied angrily.

I stood up and went over to my door. "You can go now."

She stood up and sighed. "I want you to remove that eye make-up before you come to dinner."

"Why should I?"

"Because it looks awful. It's not you, Harper, and besides Mr Wood is coming over for dinner at six o'clock. Also I would like you put on something nicer than what you wore today for the funeral."

"Like I said to Dad before, I am who I am, I'm not changing for anyone!"

"Fine, Harper, I'm not going to argue with you. I know you are upset," she said.

As she walked out, I slammed the door shut behind her and kicked it hard.

"Goddamn it!" I yelled as I got changed into the blackest outfit I had.

Walking out into the corridor, I could hear my parents talking in the sitting room. I stopped to listen to their conversation.

"I think it is time, Phil. She is saying she is seeing the shadow man again and this time it is worse: she is saying that she is having conversations with him as well."

"So then it's time?" he asked.

I could hear agitation rising in his voice.

"Maybe it would be best for her to go away for a break, to get away from all the memories here. I found a lovely place in the country, a place where children like Harper go to get better, to continue her schoolwork. She has missed out on so much already."

"So you think we should just hide her away?"

"No Phil, I don't want to hide her away, I want her to get better. She has gone through enough already. Maybe if she is around different kids, kids like her, it might do her good."

I shook my head and grabbed my coat as I stood there and listened to their pathetic conversation.

I slipped it on and walked into the lounge room.

"I'm going out," I told my parents.

"Where are you going? It's raining outside." Mother turned to me.

"Out, to clear my head. I feel so locked up in this house."

"I don't think that is a good idea, Harper. You fainted earlier, what happens if it happens again when you are out?" she asked.

"It won't," I said as I turned to leave.

"But..."

"Let her go, sweetie, she needs time, it's a good idea for her to get outside, get some fresh air."

As I made my way out the front door, I looked up to the dark sky. Rain was falling steadily from the ominous-looking clouds.

I pulled my coat tighter around me as I decided to head over to the cemetery. As I crossed over to the forest side of the street, the wind started to blow more fiercely. By the time I reached the cemetery gates, I was cold and very wet. I checked my watch. It was five thirty.

I made my way across the wet grass to where Ryan was buried. A fresh mound of dirt with a white wooden cross bearing Ryan's name marked the place where he had been laid to rest.

I sat down and picked at what was left of the grass around it.

"Hey Ryan," I began. "Sorry I bailed on you today, mother said I fainted, that would have been embarrassing, I'm glad I don't remember."

I stopped talking to the mound of dirt. The wind started howling and the rain fell harder. I stood up.

"I have to go," I said.

As I turned to leave, I noticed a figure leaning against a tree about ten graves down, watching me. I leant forward and stared though the rain trying to get a better look.

"Shit," I mumbled under my breath.

It was the smiling boy from the funeral. This was just perfect. Now what was I supposed to do?

"Don't go, Harper," a male voice whispered through the wind.

I continued staring at the mysterious stranger. He was closer now, close enough for me to see him clearly. My heart started to beat faster. Dear God, he was good-looking!

His face was pale and his lips blood-red, with piercing ice-blue eyes that were outlined in black make-up. He stood quite still, despite the strong wind blowing wildly around us.

"Do I know you?" I shouted over the howling wind.

He shook his head no, then nodded it yes.

"I should go," I told him as I took two steps back.

"Don't," he replied with force.

I stopped dead in my tracks. I didn't like the way he was glaring at me.

"I don't know what you want or who you are, but I would like to leave," I yelled over the wind.

"Hey, you there?"

I spun around to find the groundsman standing behind me, holding a shovel. He was wearing a yellow raincoat and a matching hat. He reminded me of a fisherman you see in horror movies.

"What are you doing here all alone?" he asked through his toothless gums.

What an odd question to ask. I wasn't alone.

"Oh I was talking to…" I turned around to find the smiling stranger gone.

"I think you best be getting home, missy, it's getting dark and a cemetery isn't a place for you at night," he said, looking at me strangely.

"Oh I thought a cemetery is the safest place to be," I said.

He continued to glare at me.

"Okay fine, I'm going," I said as I took one last look over my shoulder.

Where did he go? How could someone disappear so quickly? The thought sent a cold shiver down my spine.

"Well?" The groundsman prompted.

I turned around to face him. "I'm going, geez," I huffed as I walked briskly out of the cemetery, picking up the pace as I headed towards home.

As I made my way up the path towards the house, I looked up to find my mother standing on the front porch.

"Where have you been, Harper Grace O'Connor?"

Oh no, she used my full name. Not a good sign.

I stopped short in front of the steps and looked up through the rain at my mother. She was standing with her hands on her hips and frantically tapping her left foot.

"Do you know what time it is?"

I swear I could see steam escaping from the top of her head. I was too scared to lift my arm to check my watch.

I shook my head no.

"It is six thirty. Ryan's father has been here for half an hour."

A chill ran down my spine at the mention of Ryan's name.

"So? I don't have to entertain him. You are the one who asked him over to dinner," I replied.

"Get inside, Harper, and wash your face before you come to dinner. You are an absolute mess!"

With that off her chest, she turned and went back inside.

Thunder roared overhead as I made my way inside and up to my bathroom. I looked in the mirror I could see why the groundsman had been staring at me strangely. She was right; my make-up had run down my face, making me look frightful.

I washed my face with warm water, got changed into dry clothes and headed into the dining room.

"Here she is, you finally made it." Dad smiled.

"Sorry I'm late, I kind of lost track of time," I said, sitting down.

"Now I can finally serve dinner," Mother huffed.

"How are you, Harper?" Mr Wood turned to me and smiled.

I wanted to scream, loudly. This is so pathetic, the poor man buried his son today and my lame mother has to have him over for dinner.

I nodded my head, speechless.

"Harper, honey, don't tear up your napkin, dear."

I looked over at Dad. "What?"

"Your napkin, sweetie, leave it be."

I glanced down at the shredded paper napkin in front of me. "Sorry," I mumbled. I hadn't even realized I was ripping it up.

"Why is everyone so quiet?" Mother asked when she returned with an elaborate roast dinner.

Was she for real? What did she think this was, a dinner party? I looked over at Mr Wood.

He turned to me and gave me a weak smile. Poor guy.

"You are probably wondering why I agreed to come to dinner, Harper," he said.

I nodded my head, puzzled.

He reached into his jacket pocket and pulled out a small, mint-green box.

"This is for you," he said, as he slid the box over to me.

"I don't understand." I shook my head.

"Ryan was going to give this to you the night of the dance. I know he would have wanted me to give it to you now." A small smile flickered on his lips.

I could tell he was fighting back tears.

I looked back down at the box, untied the green ribbon and pulled off the lid. A black leather wrap bracelet with two small rectangle plates hanging next to each other lay on the pure white pillow. I picked it up gingerly and turned the plates over. One read 'promise' and the other 'forever'.

"Would you like me to help you put it on?" Mr Wood asked.

"Yes, please." I handed him the bracelet and held out my left wrist.

He fastened it with slightly shaking hands, then gave me a smile.

"He loved you, Harper, just so you know," he said.

"That looks special, Harper," Mother said as she began to serve dinner.

I couldn't take my eyes off the bracelet as the two words danced around in my head.

I could hear my parents talking to Ryan's dad, but their words just blended into one big blur.

Promise forever? The voice scoffed.

"What?" I looked up.

Everyone stopped talking and turned their heads my way.

"Sorry, Harper?" Mother looked at me strangely.

"What did you say?" I asked again.

"No one was talking to you, honey, we were talking amongst ourselves," Dad said, glancing from my mother to me.

I looked at Mr Wood, who nodded his head.

"Mother, can I ask you something?"

"Of course dear, what is it?"

"You know when I was three and I use to see things?"

She glanced over at Mr Wood. "I don't think now is the time, honey," she smiled.

"Well I just want to know something," I chose to ignore her.

"Harper," she warned.

If looks could kill!

"Was it a boy or a girl?" I asked, knowing full well it was a boy.

"Harper Grace, now is not the time," she said through clenched teeth.

"What? You said any time I need to talk. Mr Wood knows, right?" I turned to him. "Ryan and I talked about it all the time."

He nodded his head.

"Now isn't the right time," she repeated.

"What time is the right time? I saw somebody today at the funeral, then just now when I went down to the cemetery to be with Ryan. I think he is stalking me; this is not in my imagination."

"Harper, sweetie, listen," Dad began, pausing to find the right words. "It's been a rough few weeks for you, your mind is trying to take everything in."

I saw Mr Wood nod his head.

"May I be excused? I don't feel too well."

"You haven't even touched your dinner, Harper," Dad said.

"I'm not hungry." I stood up.

"We have company, Harper. You are being rude." Mother sighed.

"That's okay, let her go. It's been a big day for her." Mr Wood smiled at her.

"Thank you." I left the room before either of my parents could say anything else.

I went into my room and closed the door.

How my parents could even think to make me sit through dinner with Ryan's father on the day of his funeral is beyond me.

I lay down on my bed and stared at the ceiling. Time seem to tick by slowly. I could hear everyone talking in the sitting room; dinner was over.

I sat up and looked around my room. I grabbed the photo of Ryan and lay back down again. I stared at the photo for an hour, not thinking about anything else.

Sleep was what I needed.

But I couldn't sleep. Tears ran down my cheeks and my mind was racing. Visions of Ryan came flooding back to me. But it was the memory of the dark-haired stranger that my mind kept returning to.

Who was he? He couldn't possibly go to school. I'd never seen him before. Or did he? Had I been too busy with Ryan, living in our own little bubble to not notice the world around us?

Maybe he was new in town; that had to be it.

Chapter 5

Three weeks had passed since Ryan's funeral and the dinner with Mr Wood. I hadn't returned to school; I couldn't face it on my own without Ryan, couldn't face the looks, the questions and all of a sudden everyone wanting to be my friend because they felt sorry for me.

"Harper, breakfast," Mother called from down the corridor.

I pushed my bare feet into my blue slippers and dragged myself to the dining room.

"Good morning, sweetie, did you sleep well?" Dad smiled.

I shrugged my shoulders. Was it a good morning? I didn't think so. Did I sleep well? No.

I flopped down in the chair and folded my arms across my chest.

"There you go, Harper." Mother smiled as she placed a plate down in front of me.

I glanced over the two stack of pancakes topped with fresh strawberries and maple syrup. I felt my stomach knot; I couldn't eat, I was finding it hard to hold anything I ate down since the funeral. I pushed the plate as far away from me as possible.

"Harper? Is something the matter?"

I looked over at my dad.

"You have to eat, sweetie. You have lost so much weight and you are looking pale and drawn," he continued.

"Not eating is not going to bring Ryan back," Mother added tartly. "Besides, you need to go back to school. You have to finish your senior year. You'll be eighteen next week."

I looked at her, shocked. How dare she?

"He's gone, Harper," she sighed. "You need to realize this and try to move on. I'm not saying to forget about him but sweetie, you don't eat, and you lock yourself in your room all day and sit by the window as if you are waiting for him to return. You don't sleep at night. I hear you walking up and down the corridor at all hours."

"You don't need to worry, Mother."

"Yes I do. I am your mother and it is my job. Like I said, you need to go back to school. You've missed so much already."

"I can't," I muttered.

"Why not?" she asked.

I looked to my father then back to my mother.

"Because I'm scared he will be at school."

"He? He who?" she questioned.

"The boy from the funeral, the one who has been stalking me ever since."

"Oh, Harper Grace, enough." She sighed. "You need to stop this nonsense. There is no one stalking you for heaven's sake, it is all in your head," she snapped.

"Is it, though?"

"Harper," she warned.

I stood up a little too quickly and knocked over my chair.

"Where are you going, Harper?" she asked.

"To my room, to be alone," I said as I turned and walked off.

"Harper?"

I heard my father call after me. I kept walking until I was out of their sight but not out of earshot.

"Forget it, Phil, I've had enough with that child. Yes, her best friend died, and I can understand her pain, but this rubbish about someone stalking her, it's not right. I think it's time, she can finish her senior year at Ella Moore. We leave first thing in the morning."

I went into my room and slammed the door shut. "I'll give her Ella Moore," I sulked.

I didn't even know what she was talking about.

That night around eleven, there was a knock at my door. I opened my eyes and sat up. "Come in."

The door opened and Mother stepped into the room. She had a suitcase in one hand and a flyer in the other.

"Are you going somewhere?" I asked smugly.

"Pack some clothes and anything else you want to bring with you, Harper, we leave for Ella Moore at seven tomorrow."

Without offering any explanation, she placed the suitcase down and the flyer on top of it and turned and walked out of the room, closing the door behind her.

Chapter 6

A sudden tapping at my bedroom door woke me from a terrifying dream. I sat up fast and looked around my room.

"Harper, are you up?" Mother called from the other side of the door.

I glanced over at my clock. Six thirty in the morning.

The door opened slowly. Mother stepped into the room and flicked on the light, causing me to blink at the brightness.

"Really?" I asked as I rubbed the sleep out of my eyes.

"It's time to get up and get dressed." Her tone was cold and distant.

"So it wasn't a nightmare, I wasn't dreaming? You are seriously sending me to that school for freaks? Don't I get a say in this?"

"No, Harper, I think you have said enough. I'm sorry but no, no you don't." She sighed.

"I won't fit in," I argued.

"Harper, you will meet kids that are like you."

"Like me? What is that supposed to mean? You know how hard it is for me to make new friends, to fit in. Why do you think Ryan was my only friend?" I asked sulkily.

"Harper, I don't want to talk about this anymore. End of discussion. I want you to get better; my decision is final."

"But?" I protested, knowing my words were falling on deaf ears.

"Ella Moore is a lovely place; it's run like a school so you can finish your final year."

"Can I come home on weekends?"

"Unfortunately, no."

"This is so unfair!" I whined.

"Unfair? Do you want to know what is unfair?" Mother fought back. "Your behaviour at the dinner table in front of Mr Wood was unfair. Do you think he wanted to see you acting that way? He probably thinks you have flipped your lid."

"So? He can think what he wants."

She let out a long sigh. "Harper you haven't been the same since the accident, your attitude is terrible and this lull you have got yourself into isn't good."

"How do you want me to be, Mother? My best friend is dead, never coming back, you're not listening to me when I talk to you after you tell me I can talk to you about anything, and now you are shipping me off to some boarding school for freaks."

"I didn't say you were a freak, Harper."

"No, but you may as well have," I replied.

"Your father and I thought Ella Moore would be a perfect place for you. Just until you finish school, it's in the country, a new place, new people to make friends with."

"I don't need new friends," I interrupted her.

"There is a hospital wing as well."

I gave her a look. "What are you implying, Mother? That I'm suicidal?" I asked her with suspicion.

"God no, Harper, all I am saying is that Ella Moore is place where you can feel safe, to be with kids like yourself."

"You said it again; that's twice now."

"Said what, Harper?" she huffed, clearly getting frustrated.

"Like me."

"What are you talking about?"

"You said that there would be kids like me. What are you getting at?"

"All I am trying to say, Harper, is that these kids have been through some tough times. No one is going to question you, you won't have to explain your situation to anyone."

"Good, because I'm not going," I told her.

"Not going is not an option, Harper," she said as she glanced at the clock on my side table.

She picked up the suitcase and opened it on the bed. I watched the flyer float to the floor.

"I see you haven't packed?" she grumbled.

"What for? I'm not going anywhere." I looked at her.

I watched in shock as she went through my drawers, throwing random clothes into the suitcase. She zipped it up and yanked it off the bed.

"Get dressed, Harper Grace, and be downstairs ready to leave. You have five minutes. You don't want me coming in here again." She spoke sharply as she walked out of the room.

I went over to my door and slammed it shut as hard as I could, making the little trinkets on my bookcase shake.

"Great! I have no say in the matter; they are sending me to a nuthouse to be with other nuts like me!" I yelled.

"Harper Grace," Mother's ice queen voice drifted up the stairs.

I huffed as I quickly got dressed and threw open the door.

"I'm coming!" I shouted as I left my room and stomped down the stairs.

"Do you have to be so childish, Harper?" she asked, handing me my coat.

I snatched it out of her hand and slipped it on.

"Your father is waiting out front," she said as she turned to leave.

I followed behind her. I couldn't believe they were sending me away without even talking to me first.

"The hearse?"

"We don't have another car, Harper. You know that."

"We took a taxi from the hospital," I reminded her.

"That was two minutes away. Ella Moore is two hours away."

Oh great, for the love of God!

"Why not ship me off overseas? Are you sure two hours is far away enough for you?" I moaned.

"Get in the car, Harper. I'm not going to argue with you out here." She sighed.

"I am not sitting in the middle of you two for two hours. I want the window seat." I folded my arms across my chest.

"Fine, Harper," she said as she got in and slid over to the middle seat.

"All set, Harper?" Father asked.

As I got in and slammed the door shut, I looked over at him. I rolled my eyes and turned my body as best I could given the tight space and looked out the window.

"Your mother and I know this is the best for you, Harper," he began.

I shook my head. This sucked.

"It's a lovely place, Ella Moore," he continued when I didn't say anything. "It's in the country set amongst a grand forest."

"And a great place to be murdered," I said under my breath.

No one spoke for the next two long, boring hours. I watched out my window as suburbia turned to scrubland. I knew I wasn't going to see home for a long time or even be able to visit Ryan's grave.

A tear rolled down my cheek. I wiped it away quickly before my parents saw. I placed my pods in my ears and turned up the volume.

Time seemed to drag, and I swore we were going to run out of gas before we even got there.

"We shouldn't be too far now." Father broke the silence.

"Oh look! Up ahead." Mother's voice sounded a little too enthusiastic.

I removed my pods and leant forward to get a better look.

"You have got to be kidding me," I gasped.

My father slowly drove the hearse through two large wrought iron gates that did not look too inviting. Quite frankly, the whole place didn't look too inviting.

The tires crunched over the gravel covering the long circular driveway. There was nothing around for miles except the forest he had mentioned earlier.

There was nothing at all appealing about the dull, grey, oversized, gothic castle. Not even the turrets, several chimneys or ugly gargoyles that watched us from above.

It was eerie looking around the empty car park.

He let out a long, slow whistle. "What a beauty."

"You think?" I turned to him.

"The hearse fits right in here," he chuckled.

"Have a look at the size of those gargoyles up there, said to be protectors of the building," Mother added.

"Are you two done?" I looked at both of them. "This is not a field trip," I said through gritted teeth as I looked back out my window to the second floor.

I noticed a boy leaning against the window. He was watching me; a wicked half-smile crept across his lips just before he pulled away and disappeared out of sight.

Father parked the hearse at the bottom of the stone steps. We got out to find a very old woman wearing a grey shirt and long blue skirt standing with her fingers locked together in front of her. It was as if she appeared out of nowhere.

Her hair was dull grey, just like the building, and it was pulled back into a bun on the top of her head.

"Hi there," my father called cheerfully as he pulled the suitcase out of the hearse.

"Good morning, I am Ms Moore. You must be the O'Connors," she said as she looked at both my parents.

She was very well-spoken. She turned her beady grey eyes towards me.

"And you must be Harper." She paused for quite some time. "We've been expecting you."

Chapter 7

My father was the first one to take a step towards Ms Moore. "Okay, well, should we get you inside and settled?" he asked.

"That won't be necessary, Mr O'Connor." Ms Moore stopped him short. "You can say your goodbyes to Harper here."

"Oh, right, right then." He turned to me and handed over the suitcase.

My hands were shaking slightly as I took it from him.

"Be a good girl, Harper, do as you are asked and try to make some new friends, okay?" He half smiled.

I nodded my head then turned to my mother, hoping she would say this was all a huge mistake and we could go home.

"It's for the best, Harper, for you to get better. We will see you soon, I promise. If you need anything just…"

"There are no phone calls permitted at Ella Moore, in or out." Ms Moore interrupted her.

I glared at my mother. "I can't believe you are doing this to me."

"It's for the best, for your own safety," she said, as tears escaped her eyes.

"My own safety?" I repeated.

What the hell did that mean?

"Harper?"

I turned to see Ms Moore gracefully descend the steps towards me. "We need to get inside," she told me, and her stone-cold expression didn't change.

Turning to face my parents, I pleaded with my eyes for them to not leave me with this scary woman in this creepy castle.

My father shook his head as if lost for words, or was he too scared to speak in case Ms Moore bit his head off?

"We will see you soon Harper, I promise." Mother gave me a weak smile before darting her eyes to Ms Moore.

Before I could answer her, my parents got into the hearse and drove off down the gravel driveway.

I watched, horrified, as the taillights disappeared through the wrought iron gates, which closed slowly behind the hearse.

As soon as the gates shut closed, Ms Moore turned and began walking up the steps to Ella Moore.

Once she reached the door, she stopped and turned to face me. "Come along dear, I have to get you settled in before morning tea." She looked down at her pocket watch, then back up again. "Which is in fifteen minutes." She began walking again.

I looked over my shoulder at the heavy iron gates. There was no going back now. My parents had gone, and the gates were locked. I turned back around and walked through the doors of Ella Moore.

My mouth fell open as I stepped into the foyer. The grand entrance looked more like an elaborate lobby of a Victorian hotel than a foyer of a boarding school.

"The birdcage lift is out of bounds," she warned me.

I looked to my left to find an ornate white metal elevator. I nodded my head in awe. I had never seen a more beautiful place, from the polished marble floor to the embellished tapestries that hung above the elaborate stone fireplace.

I looked around the completely empty foyer. It was quiet. Where was everybody?

"Right this way, Miss O'Connor."

I followed her up the white marble staircase, her long blue skirt leading the way. Her black heels clicked loudly on every step, and I was glad when we reached the top. Deep red carpet greeted us. As I looked around, overwhelmed, Ms Moore turned to face me.

"We have strict rules here at Ella Moore. Boys to the right, girls to the left. Follow me." She continued walking.

The place was completely quiet.

I looked down at my watch. It was nine thirty. Surely people would be up and walking around by now.

Ms Moore stopped in front of a wooden door and pulled out an antique bronze key from her pocket.

"You have this room to yourself for now. Unfortunately your would-have-been roommate left us suddenly last week."

What was that supposed to mean? I thought we weren't allowed to leave.

She placed the key in the lock then pushed the heavy door open. I walked past her into the empty room.

"There is a map on your desk. Take a moment to study it. You do not want to get lost. The upstairs library is off limits, and the dining hall is downstairs." She paused and pulled out her pocket watch again. "You have three minutes before the bell, so be sure not to be late." She turned and left the room, leaving the door open behind her.

I stood there and looked around. Two beds, two desks and an empty bookshelf. I chose the bed closest to the window.

I placed my suitcase on the bed. "This isn't so bad," I tried to convince myself.

I went over to the heavy maroon drapes and pulled them open. "Wow!"

The view from my second floor window was amazing. I had a full panoramic view of the forest, a gazebo and a boy leaning against a giant willow tree, watching me.

I leant forward to get a better look when a bang out in the corridor drew my attention to the doorway.

There was nobody there, and by the time I had turned back around, the boy had disappeared.

Maybe I was seeing things; maybe it was just a shadow I had seen. Right? Isn't seeing things that weren't there what landed me in here in the first place?

I went over to the desk, picked up the map and looked for the dining hall. Ms Moore said it was downstairs. I found it and took on board that it was past the grand staircase, down an endless corridor then the third door on the right. Got it.

The bell sounded just as I placed the map back down on the desk. I left my room to be greeted by what seemed like hundreds of students, all heading in the same direction. Not one of them looked my way or even noticed I was there.

Finding the dining hall wasn't going to be a problem at all.

I fell behind three girls, all with long blonde hair and all wearing short chequered skirts topped off with extremely tight white t-shirts.

We made our way into the dining hall and lined up to get our food. I thanked the woman behind the counter as she handed me the tray. The girl in front turned to me, glared and shook her head before walking off.

I took my tray and went to find a seat, only to notice that my presence in the room had suddenly seen every vacant chair occupied by a backpack, while any free table space was now taken up by half-eaten plates of food.

I looked down at my tray and suddenly lost interest in the warm milk, the day-old berry muffin and the yellow slop that was labelled custard with fruit.

I sighed as I grabbed the apple off the tray and ditched the rest in a trash can. I found a spare table by the window, dragged out the chair and sat down.

"Sitting by yourself is a big no-no here at Ella Moore."

I looked up to find a girl with fire-red hair standing at my table.

I looked at her, confused. "Sorry?"

"You will be if you're not careful. There are rules here at Ella Moore, you know?" She sat down opposite me.

"No I didn't know," I said, watching her.

"I'm Saffron, by the way."

"Saffron?"

What an unusual name.

"Well, you can call me Sid," she beamed.

"Sid?" I repeated.

"Saffron Isobel Delaney, Sid for short." She smiled.

Her teeth were perfectly straight and gleaming white. I ran my tongue over my teeth.

"Harper." I told her.

"I know, you're new here, news travels fast."

I nodded my head and looked around at the groups of kids. Sid was right, no one was sitting by themselves, just in groups.

She saw me looking.

"Over there," she pointed. "You have your emos, they keep to themselves. Them there," she motioned her head in the other direction, "nerds, good to be friends with in case you need your laptop fixed."

"What about them?"

"Oh God, don't get me started on them." She scoffed. "Wannabe jocks and cheerleaders, the privilege kids that came from colleges that did sport. We don't do sports here, I mean can you imagine the emos playing hockey?" She laughed as she picked up a carrot stick from her tray.

I nodded my head and glanced around the room. I didn't fit in here; I wasn't an emo, a nerd or even like playing sport. Who was I going to fit in with? Where did Sid fit in?

Then suddenly someone caught my eye. Sitting alone at a table by another window was a boy dressed all in black. He could have maybe fit in with the emos but was sitting by himself. I thought Sid said that was a no-no.

I looked over his brown hair. It was longish and messy.

"Who's that?" I asked, not taking my eyes off of him.

Sid looked up and followed my stare to where I was fixed on the lone stranger.

She choked, coughing up a half-chewed carrot stick. "No, Harper, don't go there!"

"What? Why are you being so dramatic?" I couldn't take my eyes off him.

"For the love of God, child, don't look at him, don't talk to him, and don't make eye contact with him," she said in a low whisper.

He was staring straight ahead at nothing.

"That's William, the loner," she began. "He doesn't talk to anyone."

"He looks harmless. A little dark, but harmless," I said, still staring at him.

"Harper please, stay away from him," she warned again.

I turned my gaze back to Sid. "You sound a little jealous Sid, fancy William for yourself?" I teased.

"Jealous? Over William? Hell would have to freeze over first," she retorted.

"Why is he sitting by himself?" I questioned, glancing his way again.

"Umm, maybe because he is a freak! He's been at Ella Moore longer than any of us. Rumour has it he burnt down a school at night, he was a runaway, he has countless police records for what, I don't want to know. He is trouble, Harper, best you stay away from him," she said, pointing a carrot stick at me.

William was still staring straight ahead at nothing in particular. A tiny smile crept across his blood-red lips.

"I'm warning you, Harper, stay well away, don't get involved with him."

He turned his head slowly towards me and his blue eyes met mine.

It was too late. Without knowing it, I was already involved.

Chapter 8

Sid stood up from the table, glanced around the room, then turned her eyes back to mine.

"I've warned you enough, Harper."

I turned my head and looked up at her.

"Get involved with the likes of him and there will be hell to pay. Literally."

A shiver ran down my spine as she turned and walked away. I looked down at the table and sighed. It wasn't going to be easy making friends here; that was a given.

Loud chatting caught my attention. I glanced up to find the three blond girls I had seen earlier standing at my table.

"New girl," the tallest one began.

I made no response as I looked over her perfect features. Her two companions stood on either side of her; they were beautiful as well.

"You should know a few things before you get settled here," she continued after I didn't answer.

Her tone wasn't friendly, nor was the glare in her piercing green eyes.

"Let me guess? You are going to be the one that tells me, right?" I leant back in my chair and folded my arms across my chest.

"I, I wouldn't take that tone with me if I were you," she stumbled.

"No?" I asked coolly, glancing over at William, then back to Miss Bossy Boots. "Why?"

"You don't know who you are dealing with. I'm Brittney."

"I'm Harper." I cut her off.

"And I don't care." She flicked her long blonde hair over her shoulder. "See Will over there?" She pointed.

I looked to William, then back to Brittney. "Yeah?"

"Get it through that head of yours that you and William will never happen… ever!"

The girl standing to the right giggled. Brittney shot her a look and she shut up fast.

"Why should I? Are you dating him?" I smirked.

"Are you testing me?" she snarled.

I shook my head no.

"Good, you wouldn't want to, that's for sure," she spat, turning on her heels and walking off. The other two followed like lost sheep.

I looked down at the apple uneaten in my hand and sighed. Making friends was never easy for me.

"You won't make friends with Brittney and her coven, so don't even try."

I glanced up to find William had left his seat and was now standing at my table.

I sat up a little straighter. "Oh," I breathed, taken aback at how good-looking he was up close, even with all that smoky make-up around his eyes. I felt my cheeks turning red.

"Hi," he said as a to-die-for smile crept across his lips. "Mind if I sit?"

"No, no, please sit."

I looked around the room and noticed every set of eyes had turned our way.

He turned the chair around and sat on it backwards. He placed his hands on top of the backrest.

I noticed his nails were painted black and a small cross was tattooed below his knuckle on his right thumb. Maybe it wasn't a tattoo; maybe it was drawn on with a black marker.

"Does it bother you?" His voice was smooth.

I looked up and our eyes met. "Huh?"

"My tattoo, my dress sense, me? Does it bother you?"

He was to die for, that was for sure. I had never met someone so good-looking. The lure in his icy pale-blue eyes was overwhelming.

"Yes, I mean no. Your eyes are so blue," I blurted out.

"Always have been," he replied in a blunt tone.

I felt unworthy to even look at such a glorious being. No wonder Brittney wanted him all for herself.

He seemed to have a hint of an accent that made his words slide off his tongue in a most unusual way. I was at a loss; he had me smitten. I had no words, so I just smiled at him.

"You have a beautiful smile, Harper," he said, then shook his head.

"Thank you."

His blue eyes fixed on my green ones. "One thing," he began.

An uncomfortable heat began to rise up through my body. I shifted in my seat, suddenly feeling awkward.

"Stay away from Brittney and her coven, they are not to be messed with. Don't get in their way, if you do, pray that you didn't. Oh and one last thing."

"Yes?" I breathed.

He leant forward in his chair; the table shifted towards me. Actually, I think the whole room shifted.

"Best you stay away from me too... well away." A pained expression crossed his face.

Why did the room feel like it was getting smaller?

"Do we have an understanding?" he continued through clenched perfectly straight teeth.

"Yes, yes of course." I shook my head, confused.

William got up off the chair and turned it back around.

I looked around the room at all the staring eyes and gaping mouths. He was not going to embarrass me on my first day at this hellhole.

"I'm not afraid of you," I called out.

A few 'oohs' floated through the room. William turned suddenly and stared down at me.

"What did you just say to me?" he growled.

I pulled back, a little scared of the look in his eyes. "Nothing. I said nothing," I stumbled.

"Good!" he spat as he turned to leave.

I let out a big sigh, as if I was holding my breath. I watched in awe as William strolled out of the dining hall. Anyone in his path moved out of the way quick smart.

"Like Oh M Gee!"

I looked up to find a different girl at my table. "Excuse me?"

"Like, what was all that about?"

"What was what about?" I asked.

I sat looking at the most beautiful girl I had ever seen. What was with this place and beautiful people?

"Ah, that conversation between you and William? Like he never talks to anyone … like ever!"

I had never heard anyone use the word 'like' more than once in a sentence. I looked her over. Her hair was cropped, jet black, and sticking up in different directions. Her skin was pale white, like she feared the sun or something, and her eyes were an unusual shade of amber.

"Um, you're staring," she giggled.

I snapped out of my stare fest and looked into her eyes.

"I'm sorry, I'm Harp-"

"Harper, I know. I'm Willow, you're new here, news travels fast." She bounced from one foot to the other.

"Yeah, so I've heard."

"So you and Wills, what's the deal?"

"Deal? There is no deal, he made sure of that. Say, tell me about Brittney?" I asked.

"Brittney?" Willow narrowed her eyes. "What do you want to know about her?"

"What's her deal?"

Willow looked around before sitting down in the same chair William had sat on.

"Best you stay away from her, Harper."

I gave her a blank look. "What did you just say?"

"Best you stay away from her, trust me, okay? She is mean and that little coven of hers is just as bad."

My mouth dropped open.

"Why are you gaping at me like that, Harper?"

"Well, it's just that, well, William said the same thing about them."

"Of course he did. That's what we all call Brittney and her friends. It's just a name, Harper, it's not like they are actual witches or anything," she scoffed.

"Right. So is there anyone else I need to stay away from?" I sighed, getting bored of this conversation.

She looked down at her nails then up to me. "Nope, just them. I don't want to see you get hurt by her, she can't be trusted."

"Why would she hurt me?"

Willow looked around the room then leant in close.

I also leant in.

"She has been going after William for three years now. She warns all the new girls to stay away from him." She sat back in her chair and looked back at her red nails.

"Well she has nothing to worry about. William made it clear for me to stay away from him and that's what I intend to do." I sat back in my chair and folded my arms across my chest.

I hoped…

Chapter 9

After my great start to the day in the dining hall, Willow offered to take me to my first class—English.

"Well this is where I leave you, Harper, I've got science. Please remember what I said about Brittney, okay?"

I nodded my head. "Sure."

She smiled at me before walking off to her class. I pulled open the heavy wooden door and stepped into the classroom.

"Shit," I mumbled under my breath as William's blue eyes turned my way.

"Ah you must be Harper; Ms Moore said you would be arriving today. Come in, come in." The teacher spoke.

I took a few more steps forward. Everyone stared at me, making me feel as if I were standing there naked. I looked down just to make sure I wasn't.

"I'm Mr Phillips, or like most the kids call me here, Mr P. Welcome to English."

I smiled at the man standing behind the desk. He was old, wrinkled and wore thick glasses.

"Thanks," I replied politely.

"Now let's see where to put you."

We both looked around the room. My eyes fell on the empty seat next to William. Oh God, no.

"Ah, yes, there we go. You can take your seat next to William."

"But…" I hesitated.

"Mr Phillips, I have to request that she doesn't sit next to me. You know I need my space."

William's voice was smooth as velvet. I noticed a few mouths drop open and a giggle escaped from Brittney's lips.

Ignoring William's plea, Mr P turned to me. "Please take your seat, Harper."

This could not be happening! Each step I took towards William was excruciating. His eyes felt like they were burning a hole right through me.

I slid into my seat and faced the front. I felt William's eyes still on me, watching me.

Mr Phillips began talking but his words were hazy, far away. I shook my head as I watched the words he wrote on the board bleed into each other. I shook my head again; what was wrong with me? I could feel William staring at me. An uncomfortable heat began to rise in me again.

I stood up a little too quickly, knocking the books off my desk.

The teacher stopped talking and everyone turned around and looked my way.

"Freak," Brittney hissed.

"Harper?"

The room began to spin wildly.

"Harper dear, are you all right?" Mr Phillips asked.

I couldn't focus.

"I need to leave," I told him.

Some of the class began to giggle and make snide remarks as I rushed out of the room into the corridor and straight into someone's chest. Ricocheting backwards, they caught me by my arm.

"Whoa, slow down. What's the hurry?" he laughed.

I looked up into what I thought was the face of an angel. He was beautiful; his hair was the colour of sand, messy, and fell across his forehead, covering his eyebrows. His eyes reminded me of my mother's, sparkling green, his lips full and red, and his skin flawless.

He was still holding my arm as I took a step back into the closed door.

"I'm sorry, I, I didn't see you there."

That would have been the most stupid thing to have said considering he was about six feet tall!

"Obviously." He laughed, pulling me gently towards him away from the door. "I'm Nathaniel."

I felt my heart began to beat fast and my breathing was coming in a little too quick. The door opened and Mr P stuck his head out.

"Oh Nathaniel, you decided to join my class. Harper, are you okay?"

"Yes, sir, thank you. Just feeling a little light-headed."

"I was just telling Harper I could take her to the infirmary, get one of the nurses to check her over."

"Yes, yes, that would be a smart idea." Mr P nodded, then headed back inside.

Nathaniel looked back down at me as he let go of my arm. "It's okay, take a deep breath. Where were you going in such a hurry like that?" he enquired, glancing over his shoulder towards the door.

"Anywhere but in there," I said.

He held out his left hand. "Come with me, I know a place." His eyes bore into mine.

I lost all train of thought as I held my hand out to him. As soon as my hand touched his, a bolt of electricity ripped through my body.

A small gasp escaped my lips. "Where are we going?"

He gave me a crooked smile. "Upstairs," he said as he pulled me down the corridor a little too quickly.

I pulled him to a stop.

"What?" His crooked smile turned into a wicked grin.

Knowing the boys dorms were upstairs, I began to worry.

"Shouldn't we be getting back to class?"

Nathaniel took a step closer to me. "Harper, this is a school for misfits. We are here to be babysat, not get an education." He laughed, as he began pulling me down the corridor.

"Wait, stop." I pulled my hand out of his, and the buzz of electricity subsided.

"I am not a misfit and how did you know my name? I never told you."

"Mr P said your name," he said bluntly, watching me.

"Oh."

Nathaniel picked up my hand and turned my wrist over. I yanked it out of his cold hand.

"What are you doing?" I asked suspiciously.

"Why are you here, Harper?" he asked, ignoring my question.

My brain clicked into overdrive and I felt a need to answer his question as his green eyes looked into mine.

"My parents thought it would be a good idea for me to get away for a while, to come here to be with kids like me. So far no one here is like me."

"Like you?"

"That's what my mother said," I replied.

He leant a little closer. "There is a reason why you are here, isn't there, Harper?"

I felt my eyes begin to burn. I wasn't going to tell him about Ryan; how I lost my only friend, ending up here in this school full of nutcases. Tears fell down my burning cheeks.

Nathaniel reached up and touched the side of my face. A sense of calmness washed over me as I felt myself melting into the palm of his hand.

I looked up into his eyes. What was the chances of two drop-dead gorgeous guys showing an interest in me? It must be because I was the new girl.

Maybe I did belong here. Maybe my mother was right.

"I should get back," I told him.

We walked side by side, not talking, back to the classroom. Suddenly I felt dizzy; it felt as if the room was getting smaller again.

"Harper? Are you okay?" Nathaniel asked.

I nodded my head. "I have to go."

Nathaniel was going in and out of focus; I turned around. There standing in the corridor was William. He was leaning against the lockers, his eyes fixed on mine.

Go. Now. The voice in my head ordered.

I couldn't breathe. I looked back at Nathaniel. His arms were folded against his chest and the glare in his eyes was mesmerizing. But I could see that the glare wasn't intended for me; it was for William.

I was going to faint and it felt like neither one of them knew I was standing between them.

There was nothing left to do except close my eyes and fall.

Chapter 10

Note to self: fainting in the middle of two hot guys on the first day at Ella Moore is not a good way to fit in.

"Do you think she did it on purpose, fainting in front of Will and Nate like that?"

Oh dear God, the humiliation.

"Well, yeah, of course."

I lay still and kept my eyes closed, trying hard to slow down my breathing. The cold, hard floor was still beneath me.

"Shut up, Brittney. Take your little coven and move on," a male voiced hissed.

Was that Nathaniel or William? I couldn't tell. *Please, please don't let it be either of them.*

I heard whispering and the shuffling of shoes moving away. I prayed that they had all gone.

"Harper, are you okay?" A soft voice whispered close to my ear, making me feel as if I was melting into the floor.

I opened my eyes slowly. There on the floor beside me, leaning in close to my face, was Nathaniel.

I tried to sit up but fell into his arms instead.

"Whoa, take it easy girl, you may have bumped your head." He smiled.

His breath brushed my face, sending a scent of peppermint candy through my lungs. I inhaled deeply.

I looked around the now-empty hall, and then back to his green eyes.

"Where's William?" I asked as I pulled myself out of Nathaniel's arms and into a sitting position.

A pained expression crossed Nathaniel's face. He closed his eyes and took in a deep breath, then opened them again. He stood up and pulled me up off the floor.

"I should take you back to your room."

"No, thank you. It's okay, I can go back on my own."

"You sure? I don't mind."

I nodded my head. I couldn't work out why someone as good-looking as Nathaniel would ever talk to me or even look my way. No one ever showed an interest in me back home, only Ryan.

Tears filled my eyes at the very thought of him.

"Harper?" Nathaniel reached for my hand. "Why are you crying?" His voice was so soothing.

I wiped away my tears with my free hand. "It's nothing," I lied as I tried to control the tears that were determined to flow.

A hint of a smile crossed his lips.

"Why are you smiling?" I asked.

"It's nothing," he began. "Well no, it's just that I've never met anyone like you, Harper, ever."

Ever was being a bit dramatic, I thought to myself.

"I'm going to go," I told him as I took a couple of steps back.

"Sure," he smiled, watching me.

I turned and headed for my room. I didn't like the way he was looking at me. As I climbed the marble staircase, I glanced back over my shoulder. Nathaniel was watching me, the creepy smile still on his lips. I made my way up the stairs a little quicker.

Throwing open the door to my room, I stepped inside.

"Hey there, Harper."

Startled, I slammed the door shut a little too hard. Standing in the middle of the room was William.

"What are you doing in here?" I asked, looking him over.

He glanced to the closed door then back to me. "I take it you are alone?"

"Yes," I exhaled. "Why wouldn't I be?"

William didn't answer me; he just took four slow and graceful steps towards me.

When he stopped within inches from my face, a slight shiver ran down my spine.

He was so handsome. I could barely look at him without blushing, or my heart picking up speed.

"Why do you wear all that eye make-up?" I asked.

He took another step closer; his body was within inches of touching mine.

"Because it's me," he whispered, causing my stomach to drop.

I looked past his lips and into his dreamy blue eyes. "Why do I get the feeling you and I have met before?"

"We haven't," he said, as he ran the back of his hand down my face. "You need to stay away from me."

"I'm not afraid of you, William," my voice quivered.

He leant forward and placed his lips close to my ear. "You should be," he whispered as his lips ever so lightly brushed against it.

The tension that was building between us was unbearable. I took a step back and looked into his eyes.

"I'm not scared of you," I lied. Quite frankly, the pull he had over me had me petrified.

He ran his hand through his hair and gave me a wicked smile. As he did, his sleeve moved up his arm.

Another tattoo, this time on the inside of his wrist. I was feeling light-headed; I couldn't take much more of his perfection standing so close to me.

"What do you want, William?"

"Just to see if you were alone. I don't want you hanging around with Nathaniel."

"Well, you can see that I am alone and that clearly Nathaniel isn't here."

"Clearly," he repeated.

"You told me I have to stay away from you," I felt my heart tightening.

"And that's what you should do."

"Well, it's a bit hard for me to do that when you are in my room, standing so close to me."

"I don't want to stay away from you." He frowned, as if the words pained him.

"I don't understand, William. You say one thing, then you say another."

"I just want to make sure you and I have an understanding,"

I couldn't blink. The hold he had over me was strong. "An understanding about what, William?" My heart was beating fast.

"I shouldn't be around you," he said. His voice was low.

A sudden urgency to have his lips on mine washed over me. I wanted him to hold me, to kiss me. "You are around me now," I whispered.

He stumbled backwards away from me; he clenched his fists tight, causing his knuckles to turn white.

"William?"

He shook his head, not looking at me. "Don't," he warned. "I have to leave. Please just stay away from me."

He pushed me aside as he rushed out of the room, slamming the door shut behind him.

Chapter 11

The next day came around a little too quickly.

I got out of bed and went over to the mirror. I looked awful. Dark circles had formed under my tired eyes. Dreams of Nathaniel and William fighting for supremacy played over and over again.

I got dressed quickly and headed out into the noisy corridor.

"Hey Harper, there you are."

I looked around to find Willow waving as she made her way over to me.

She came up and wrapped her arms around me tight. I wasn't used to this kind of affection.

"Where have you been, girl? You missed dinner last night." She smiled as she pulled away from me.

"Yeah, I had a headache, must have hit my head hard when I fainted," I lied.

"Yeah well, you look like crap, no offence." She laughed.

I smiled at her. "None taken," I said as I looked around the hallway. "Say Willow, before we go down to breakfast, can I ask you something?"

"Sure Harper, is everything okay?"

"I'm not sure, it's about William."

She raised an eyebrow at me. "Harper?"

"I know you told me I should stay away from him, but there is something that just pulls me towards him every time."

"He's hot?" She cut me off, not letting me finish.

"Yeah that too, but also…"

"He is beyond handsome?" She raised her eyebrows up and down.

I couldn't help but laugh at her. "Yeah, he is."

There was no point in even trying to explain to her what I felt every time I was around William; clearly, she just wasn't getting it.

"Listen, just be careful okay? I know he is to die for, but there is something about William that I just can't put my finger on. Guys like him don't normally talk to girls like us. You are the new girl here, the shiny new toy. Just be careful is all I'm saying, okay?"

I nodded my head but had no idea what she was talking about.

She linked her arm through mine. "Come on." She beamed as she pulled me down the corridor to the dining room.

The room was already full by the time Willow and I lined up. I looked around. To my disappointment, William was nowhere to be seen.

"You'll find he doesn't always do breakfast," Willow said as if reading my mind.

I chose to ignore your comment. "You know, Willow, I'm not that hungry. Maybe I'll just sit with you."

"You should always eat breakfast, Harper," a male voice said from behind me.

I turned around to find Nathaniel standing there.

Willow nudged me a little too hard with her elbow, causing me to take a step closer to Nathaniel. What was she doing? I just finished telling her I liked William. I turned to her and gave her look to tell her I wasn't very impressed, then turned back to Nathaniel.

"Sorry about that," I shook my head. "What were you saying?"

"You should always eat breakfast," he said and smiled before walking away.

As he walked off, I noticed his hands were empty.

I turned back to face Willow, who was standing there, gaping at me.

"Ah hello?" she said.

"What?"

"You and I need to talk."

I followed her over to an empty table and sat down.

"Spill," she said.

"Spill what?"

"Nathaniel, like hello? I have never seen him speak to anyone."

"I don't know." I shrugged.

"You mean to tell me that you have both Nathaniel and William, the only two hottest guys in this hellhole, talking to you?"

"I guess."

"You guess?" she repeated.

I was losing my patience with her short questions. "What seems to be the problem, Willow? I'm not understanding."

She moved her tray to one side, forgetting about her breakfast and leant across the table to be closer to me.

"So tell me, Harper, how'd you do it?" she whispered.

"Do what?"

"Get both of the hottest guys in here to talk to you? They hardly speak to the teachers, let alone us common folk."

"Say, Harper?" A singsong voice interrupted our conversation. Both Willow and I looked up.

"What do you want, Brittney?" Willow beat me too it.

"A word with Harper," Brittney hissed.

"Go on," I said, folding my arms across my chest.

Brittney placed her hands palm down on the table and leant in close to my face. "I saw William leave your room last night."

I felt myself smirking. "And?"

"And, you tell me? Why was he in your room? He's not allowed in your room?" Her voice croaked.

I glanced past her and saw William stroll into the dining hall. My heart skipped a beat.

"He's here now," I said as I looked back at her. "Go ask him yourself."

Her cheeks turned bright red. "I, I won't do such a thing! Just stay away from him."

"I'll stay away from him if he stays away from me," I told her.

She backed away from the table, shocked. "I have warned you, Harper." She turned and walked off.

As I watched her leave the room, I caught a half-smile on William's lips.

I sat back in my chair and sighed. "What is it with this place?"

"It will get better. It doesn't help that you have caught the attention of the two guys that all the girls are trying to win over." She smiled.

I smiled back at her. She glanced past my shoulder and stood up quickly.

"I have to go," she blurted out, picking up her bag and hurrying out of the room.

I shook my head. If the morning could get any weirder, it would.

"I didn't mean to scare her off."

And it just did.

I turned in my seat to find William standing there. My stomach knotted.

"Mind if I sit?" he asked.

"No, you can sit." I watched him as he made his way over to the chair Willow had just been sitting in.

"I thought I had to stay away from you?" I treaded lightly.

"You do. But I don't," he replied coolly.

"That doesn't make any sense." I shook my head at him, not being able to take my eyes off his.

"Here's the thing," he began. "You are not good for me. I can barely control myself when I am around you. I don't know why; this has never happened to me before."

I could feel my cheeks turning red. "Control yourself?"

"Trust me, okay? I'm not good for you, Harper. I need you to do me a favour."

"Anything," I replied.

"Don't look at me, don't talk to me and don't think about me, try and keep your thoughts to yourself, okay?"

Keep my thoughts to myself? What did he mean by that?

"You are making it hard for me to do that William," I said.

He shook his head. "Why did you come here?"

"What?"

It was the same question Nathaniel asked me yesterday.

"Just answer the question. You are almost eighteen." He closed his eyes, then opened them again.

"What has that got to do with anything? What does it matter why I am here? Why are you here? Why is Willow here?"

He closed his eyes again, then took in a deep breath and opened them.

"Just stay away from me," he said through tight lips.

"Tell me why, William?" I begged.

I could see it pained him every time I said his name.

He slammed his fist down on the table. "Just do as I say, okay?" he snarled.

"Fine."

"Oh and one other thing, Harper."

I looked into his eyes.

"Stay away from Nathaniel too, he really isn't a good fit for you."

With that said, he stood up and walked away from me.

"My, my. Had a little tiff with William, I see?"

I looked up to find Brittney had edged her way back to my table. "What do you want now, Brittney?" I sighed. I was getting quite tired of her in my face all the time.

"Just making sure you understood what I said a moment ago."

"Well you can see he's not here, doesn't that tell you something?"

"Just stay away from him, okay?" Her voice quivered. She began to walk away. Was she going to cry? Oh, this just got better.

"Say, Brittney?" I called to her.

She stopped and turned around. I stood up. She had just upped the stakes; this was war. A few people had turned their eyes our way.

"William, he's not taken, you know. I'd say he is fair game," I said as I pushed past her, leaving her standing there with her mouth wide open in shock.

Chapter 12

The bell finally sounded for the last time that day. It was Friday, the end of the school week.

I left English class, relieved that William hadn't shown.

"Say, Harper?"

I looked across the hall to see Nathaniel casually leaning against the wall. He brought his hand up and ran it through his sandy blonde hair as he strolled over to me.

"Hey," I smiled.

"It's the weekend." He told me as if I didn't know.

"Yes, it is." I nodded.

"So would you like to hang out… with me… this weekend?"

A few lingering bodies turned their heads in our direction. Nathaniel took a step closer to me.

"It isn't a trick question, Harper. I won't hurt you," he whispered.

What an odd thing to say. I glanced around the room and saw people still staring. What was with everyone in this school?

"Let's walk," I replied as I moved away from prying eyes.

Nathaniel quickly caught up to my side. "I know a place we can go, to be alone," he murmured close to my ear.

I stopped walking and looked up at him. "Excuse me?"

"The gazebo, outside." He smiled.

I nodded my head and began walking again.

We stepped outside. The sun was shining, and it was a beautiful day with a bright clear sky.

A couple sitting on the lawn under the big oak tree looked up at us in amazement as we walked past.

"Ignore them," Nathaniel said, "it just isn't worth it."

I nodded my head. Why was everyone being like this? Who was Nathaniel? Why did everyone treat him like he was untouchable? William too.

"You doing okay?" Nathaniel asked as we crossed the lawn.

"Yeah, why?" I questioned as I stepped into the gazebo.

"Just making sure, that's all. I've seen Brittney hovering a bit and I'm pretty certain it's not to make friends."

I sat down on the green wooden bench and Nathaniel sat down close to me. His knee brushed up against mine every now and then.

"Yes, you are right. She has made it very clear I wouldn't be joining their little threesome anytime soon." I smiled at him.

Nathaniel picked up my hand and entwined his cool fingers between mine.

"The other day," he began, "you were crying, is everything okay?" He turned to look at me.

"Yeah, I guess I'm finding it a little hard to fit in."

"You fit in fine with me."

The butterflies took flight in my stomach again.

"Why are you being so nice to me, Nathaniel?"

Without saying a word, his free hand reached up and caressed the side of my face. I closed my eyes and leant into his hand.

Opening my eyes again, I looked into his, searching them for answers. He brought down his hand.

"Tell me about him?"

"Him? Him who?" Puzzled, I shook my head.

"Ryan. The other day you mentioned his name. Is he your boyfriend?"

Did I mention his name? Honestly, I couldn't remember.

"He was my friend, my best friend. We were going to the school dance together," I paused, trying to fight back tears.

"Go on," he pushed.

I looked at him. Had his eyes turned a little darker?

"There was an accident," I swallowed hard as the images of that night raced through my mind.

"We don't have to talk about it if it upsets you too much."

"He was my best friend and he died." I gripped Nathaniel's hand tighter; the pain of retelling the story was almost unbearable.

"It was raining, Ryan lost control of the car, it flipped and landed on its roof. Ryan died instantly. I somehow made it out alive with only a couple of scratches and a mild concussion. Go figure." I released my grip on his hand.

Nathaniel moved closer to me and pulled me into his arms. He held me tight. It felt so good. "I'm so sorry, Harper."

It felt comforting to have his strong arms around me. I inhaled deeply, taking in his peppermint scent.

I pulled away and gazed into his eyes.

"What?" he asked, smiling.

Without saying anything, I leant forward and placed my lips on his. Nathaniel opened his mouth, welcoming my kiss.

Stop, Harper! The voice in my head screamed.

I closed my eyes tighter and pulled Nathaniel closer to me, picturing Ryan, kissing him, devouring him and receiving the same response from him.

I lifted his t-shirt a little and ran my hands over his lower back. His cool skin made my warm fingers tingle.

As I started to move my hands up his back, he pulled away quickly.

"Wait, Harper, not out here," he said.

Looking at him bewildered, I shook my head.

"Nathaniel, I'm so sorry. I don't know what came over me. I'm not like this, honest." I slid away from him, disgusted with myself.

"Harper, it's okay, I liked it." He smiled.

"You did?"

"Yeah, I did. Just not here, not with all these people watching."

I looked around the garden. He was right; half the student body was watching us. I felt my cheeks burn. Nathaniel stood up and stretched. I looked up at him.

"Are you leaving?" I asked disappointed.

"I um, I forgot I have a meeting with Ms Moore in fifteen minutes. I guess I'll see you later?" he said as he almost tripped down the steps of the gazebo.

So much for spending the weekend together. *You happy now, Harper? Throwing yourself at Nathaniel like that?* I thought to myself.

I watched him as he took off across the lawn, almost running. I watched him until he disappeared inside.

I brought my fingers to my lips, which were still tingling. Why did it feel like I was kissing Ryan? What had I done? I couldn't believe I'd scared him off.

I sat alone in the gazebo while everyone around me sat in pairs or groups, enjoying the sunshine.

This was plain torture. I buried my face in my hands.

"Harper? Are you all right?"

I looked up to find William gracefully climbing the steps. His heavy combat boots made no sound.

He came and sat down next to me.

Was I magnet for these two?

"Hey." I faked a smile. I wasn't in the mood for a real one.

He took my hand in his. "Hey yourself." He smiled back.

I looked at our hands, then up to his fascinating blue eyes.

"You are wearing less eye make-up today." I remarked, treading lightly, not wanting to scare him off too.

A small laugh escaped from his mouth.

"I thought it might make me less scary."

"You're not scary," I replied.

"No?"

"Not at all. Different maybe, but not scary."

"Different, hmm, I like that."

As William looked down at our interlaced fingers, his hair fell across his face. I reached up with my free hand and brushed it back. He looked up into my eyes.

"I'm so sorry, Harper," he whispered.

"For?"

The beat of my heart picked up as William slid closer to me. I quickly stood up and went over to the other side of the gazebo. Within seconds, William was standing in front of me. He placed his hands on my waist.

Seconds passed, feeling like minutes. I looked into his eyes.

"Your hands are on my hips," I informed him, in case he wasn't aware of it.

"I know, and now my lips are going to be on yours." He pulled me in closer to him and our lips almost touched.

My heart smashed against my chest; the heat was rising again. I could feel my blood rushing through my veins.

"Harper," he exhaled, his warm breath brushing my face.

"I'm here."

William pushed me back, pinning me against the rail, his lips crashing into mine. The urgency in his kiss was overwhelming.

I placed my hand on his chest.

That was odd; why wasn't his heart beating as fast as mine? I pushed him back a little, stopping our kiss. He cocked his head to the side, his crooked smile returning.

"I don't understand you. You tell me to stay away, yet..." My heart was beating way too fast, and I couldn't control my breathing.

William closed the gap between us and placed his cool finger on my throbbing lips.

"Shh," he whispered as he nodded his head, turned and walked out of the gazebo.

Chapter 13

I stood, once again alone in the gazebo. All I could think of was what just happened between William, Nathaniel and me.

When I kissed Nathaniel, why did I feel like I was kissing Ryan; no, I was sure I was kissing Ryan. Why did two of the hottest guys here both want my attention, me, plain Jane, the girl next door?

When I kissed William, my body felt like it was on fire, the urgency in his kiss, his hands on my hips. His dark and mysterious nature lured me towards him every time, his blue eyes, that kiss. My stomach knotted at the very thought of his lips on mine, the way he looked at me, the way his words rolled smoothly of his tongue.

Mmm… his tongue, the way it darted in and out of my mouth.

But then there was Nathaniel, his green eyes, his flawless skin.

Loud thunder roared overhead, snapping me out of my daydream.

I hurriedly made my way out of the gazebo and halfway across the lawn when lightning lit up the sky. I watched as everyone around me rushed inside to shelter. I picked up the pace a little as the first few drops of rain fell from the dark storm clouds above.

How could the weather change so quickly? The storm seemed to come out of nowhere.

As I stepped into Ella Moore, I was startled to find Willow standing there frantically tapping her left foot.

"Hey there," I smiled as I brushed some raindrops off my shoulders.

"Hey there? Is that all you have to say?" she asked angrily.

An uneasy laugh escaped from my mouth. "What?"

"I have been looking all over the school for you. Do you have any idea how worried I've been? Then to find you out in the gazebo with him!"

"Aren't you being a bit dramatic, Willow?"

"Me dramatic? Throwing yourself at Nathaniel is being dramatic, don't you think, Harper?"

"You saw?" I blushed.

"Ah yeah, like the whole school saw."

What was her problem? Wasn't she the one that elbowed me closer to him in the dining hall?

"So I kissed him, what's the big deal?"

Willow's mouth dropped open. "You cannot be serious?"

She looked around the empty foyer, grabbed my arm and pulled me towards the marble staircase.

"You have no idea why you are here, do you?" she huffed, pulling me a little faster.

"What are you talking about? Where are you taking me?"

"Upstairs. It's time you and I talked."

Willow dragged me upstairs and along the corridor.

"Where are we going?" I asked, almost out of breath.

Without stopping, she said, "To the old library, I have to show you something."

We headed towards another flight of stairs. These ones were wooden and looked old and rickety. Was she for real?

"I can walk by myself, Willow," I said as I tried to shake her hand off my arm.

She stopped walking and turned to me. "You won't run off?"

"Where would I go that you won't find me?"

She thought about it for a moment, then shrugged her shoulders. "Point taken." She let go and my arm fell to my side. Willow was watching me with caution.

"It's okay," I assured her. "I'm not going to run. Now what is it you want to show me?"

She didn't answer me as we entered the empty library. The smell of dust and mould was overwhelming.

My hand went straight to my nose. "Geez, it stinks in here, are we meant to even be up here?"

"No, so don't go blabbing to anyone that you were, especially not Nate or Will." She turned and glared at me.

"Okay, I wasn't going to, relax."

"This way, over here," she said as we walked further into the room.

I looked around the massive library. It was actually quite beautiful except dust had settled on everything: desks, books and shelves. Why would all these books still be in here if no one used it? Why would the room be unlocked if no one was allowed in here?

"Harper, over here," she whispered, almost scaring me.

I hadn't realized I was lagging behind. I moved quicker to catch up with her.

As we rounded yet another dusty bookshelf, my breath caught in my throat.

"Oh wow!"

What stood before us was a magnificent floor-to-ceiling stained-glass window.

Willow came and stood next to me. "So what do you think?" she asked.

I was transfixed by the beautiful rainbow of colours of the two angels embedded in the glass.

"Do you believe in angels, Harper?" The tone in her voice was serious.

I pulled my eyes off the magnificent image and looked at her blankly.

"What?" I laughed, uneasy.

"Angels. Do you believe in them?"

"No."

"Are you sure about that?" she persisted.

"Is that why you dragged me up here into this stinking, dusty room? Just to ask me if I believed in angels? You are kidding me, right?"

Willow glanced up at the window, then back down to me.

"You don't get it, do you?" she asked.

"Get what?"

"Why you are here. You haven't been told, have you?"

"Told what?"

"What I'm about to tell you cannot be repeated. Do you understand?"

"Yes, Willow, I understand." I smiled, humouring her.

"See the angels in the glass?" she began.

I looked up to the two angels and really saw them for the first time. The window wasn't magnificent or beautiful after all. Suddenly I saw the darkness behind the image and shuddered at what I was looking at.

One of the angels, the one with the white wings, was standing over the black-winged angel, who was sprawled out on the green grass. The white-winged angel had his foot on the other angel's chest, pinning him down. The one standing held a spear above his head, ready to strike the one on the ground. Black feathers lay strewn everywhere.

I shuddered. "And?" I murmured.

"The angel that is holding the spear, he is the good guy," she began as she watched me carefully.

"That is ridiculous! How can he be the good guy if he is stepping on the other one, ready to kill him?"

"The other angel, the one with the black wings, is bad— very bad."

This was silly. What did this have to do with anything? What was Willow getting at?

"A bad angel?" I turned to her.

"Yes."

"That's stupid, there is no such thing."

"Really? Have you not heard of Satan, Harper?"

A cold chill ran down my spine as Satan and my name were mentioned in the same sentence.

"Of course I have."

"Well, Satan is a fallen angel. He is known as the deceiver who leads humans astray. The angel with the white wings is the good guy trying to destroy the evil one."

I couldn't help but smile. The seriousness on her face was too much.

"You're joking, right? You mean to tell me you dragged me up here to tell me that?"

Willow looked around the empty room then took a step closer to me.

"We are all here for a reason, Harper, and obviously you haven't been told why. Be careful of Will and Nate, think carefully about what I just told you. They are not the only ones, but they are the only ones you need to be wary of."

I looked at her blankly. Was she for real?

"What I have just told you doesn't leave this room or your lips. Do you understand?"

The hairs on my arms began to tingle because of how she was looking at me. No, I didn't understand.

I nodded my head anyway.

"Stay away from the both of them," she urged as she turned to leave.

"Willow, wait." I called after her.

She stopped and turned back around.

"I want to tell you something."

"I think we should leave, Harper."

"It's about William."

Willow took a step closer to me and placed her hand on my shoulder.

"I know what you are going to say, Harper, but it isn't wise for either of you. You are here for a reason, but I am not the one who can tell you why."

"What do you mean? You are not making any sense."

"It's too dangerous for all of us."

Fear swept over me. What was she talking about? What did she mean why I was here? My best friend died, I wasn't coping, I tried to talk to my mother about the voice I was hearing then I ended up here, in a school for deranged kids. It was becoming clear to me that this wasn't a school; it was a home for the unusual.

A dark shadow moved in front of the window outside, making both of us jump. A look of horror crossed Willow's face.

"We need to leave now." She began walking away.

"Willow, I think I'm in love with William," I blurted out.

"You what?" She stopped and turned to face me.

"I'm not sure, it's just that both Nathaniel and William, well..."

"Wait, what?" Willow shook her head.

"They are both being so kind to me. I don't have any friends here, Willow."

"So you go and make friends with two of the most wicked guys in school?" Her breathing picked up as she spoke.

"Wicked? What are you...?"

A loud bang outside the library door stopped me from continuing.

"You need to stay away from both of them."

"I don't know if I can," I said.

"Harper..."

Another bang, louder this time.

"We need to go," Willow said as she hurried me out of the library.

We rushed through the hall, down the wooden stairs and back to my room.

"Do you want to come in?" I asked as I opened the door.

I didn't want to be alone in this creepy building; Willow had given me the creeps with all that angel talk in that disgusting library. Willow glanced over my shoulder, then back to me.

She shook her head. "It's best if I don't. I have to go," she said as she turned and hurried off.

Chapter 14

I stepped into the room and closed the door behind me.
"God that was weird."

"Weird isn't the half of it."

"Shit?" Startled, I looked up to find Nathaniel standing by the window. He was twirling a black feather between his fingers, kind of like the black feathers that were in the stained glass. I shuddered at the thought.

"Sorry, Harper, I didn't mean to startle you," he said as he put the feather down on the desk.

"It's okay, I was out talking to…"

"Willow, I know."

"You do?"

Nathaniel moved a little too quickly across the room and came and stood within inches of my face.

"How do you…?"

"Shh," he whispered, placing a cool finger on my warm lips. "You ask too many questions."

"Well I have more questions for you, like how do you get in here when the door is locked?"

"Does it matter?" He tilted his head to the side.

"Yeah, it kind of does. It's a little creepy that you can come in here like that."

"Question two?" He smirked, ignoring me.

"Why me? Why not Brittney or any other girl that is way prettier than me?"

Nathaniel pushed me back a little, taking me by surprise.

"I don't want Brittney," he replied, smiling as he pushed me again. I stumbled back.

With each step he took towards me he breathed, "I... want... you." He gave me a final push, which landed me on the bed.

Within seconds he was on the bed next to me, his green eyes ablaze.

How did he move so quickly? My heart began to beat fast.

Nathaniel placed his hand on my knee before running it slowly up my thigh.

"It's not difficult to understand, Harper. I like you. I want to take you out for dinner tonight," he said.

I shook my head at how he changed direction with his question. "Dinner?"

He moved closer to me. "Just you and me, away from this place," he whispered in my ear.

I laughed uneasily. "Where would we go?"

"I've made plans, with Ms Moore," he said as his hand made its way to the top of my jeans.

I was finding it very hard to control my breathing.

"Is that a tattoo?" he asked, looking cheekily into my eyes.

Before I could register another change in conversation, Nathaniel had his hand on my t-shirt.

In all the confusion of him pushing me I hadn't realized my t-shirt had ridden up when I landed on the bed.

A wicked smile crossed his lips as he raised my t-shirt higher.

I grabbed his wrist as his cool fingers ran over the outline of the butterfly tattoo, causing my whole body to tingle.

"How did you get a tattoo at only seventeen?" He looked into my eyes, still tracing the outline.

"Hawaii," I exhaled at the elation that was running through my body.

"Oh, right. They have a no age limit there, do they?"

I closed my eyes, letting the exhilarating sensation of his cool fingers drag over my skin.

"Mmm hmm," I murmured, not really caring. I opened my eyes and looked at him.

"It's very sexy," he purred.

I looked at his lips. He was driving me crazy.

"I want to kiss you, Harper."

My heart felt as though it had dropped to the floor. I had never met anyone like Nathaniel before.

Before today I'd never kissed a boy, let alone been in a situation like this. He moved his body closer to me and then leant in.

Don't do it, Harper, the voice in my head whispered.

He gently placed his lips on mine. "Close your eyes," he ordered.

I did as he asked.

A sudden urgency to have him overcame me. I pulled him in closer to me.

He gave in and his body relaxed as he kissed me harder.

I lifted his t-shirt and began to run my hands up his cool back.

"No, don't." He blurted out between kisses.

He reached back and grabbed my wrists, pinning them above my head.

I tried to wriggle out of his strong hold, failing miserably. I turned my head to the left as he continued to kiss my neck.

"Mmm, I never knew you could taste this good, Harper."

My insides turned to jelly.

"Nathaniel, stop, please."

He pulled himself away and sat up. I sat up too, pulling my t-shirt down.

"Shit." He sighed as he ran his hand through his hair.

I sat there feeling numb, staring at him. The whole time he was kissing me, thoughts of William ran wild in my mind. I shook my head.

"Harper, I am so sorry."

"It's okay," I told him.

"No, no it's not okay, you don't deserve to be treated like that. I don't know what came over me, the urgency to kiss you, I've never felt like that before." He looked down at me.

I reached out, placed my fingers under his chin and lifted his face up. Our eyes met.

"Nathaniel, it's okay, you stopped when I asked you to stop."

He gave me a melting smile. "Can we take it slow? I like you, Harper."

"I like you too, Nathaniel."

As the words left my lips, I felt bad. Did I like him? Or was it William I desired? Why did I lose all train of thought around him? Why did I envision William when I was kissing Nathaniel?

"So are we still on for dinner?" He smiled.

"Yes, dinner would be good." I smiled back.

I watched as he got off the bed.

"I haven't scared you off, have I?" he asked as he cocked his head slightly.

I looked up at him. "No, Nathaniel, not at all."

"Great. I'll meet you in the foyer at seven?"

"Seven it is."

He nodded and made his way out of the room.

I fell back down on the soft pillow and smiled. Was Nathaniel wicked like Willow said? Yes, probably in lots of ways, but somehow I didn't think that was what she was talking about. I glanced over at the clock and jumped out of bed.

What? How did it get to six thirty? Great, not only did I lose my train of thought around Nathaniel, I lost time as well.

I raced around the room, throwing off my clothes, and then pulled on my black skinny-leg jeans and black long-sleeved tee.

I opened the door slowly, hoping no one was in the corridor. To my great relief, there was no one around. I stepped out and quietly closed the door.

I quickly made my way downstairs. A smile crossed my face when I saw Nathaniel standing in the foyer.

I made my way over to him.

"Hey, beautiful."

"Hi." I blushed.

He held out his hand to me and I placed my hand in his.

Don't do it, Harper. The voice whispered in my head.

"Ready?" He smiled.

"Sure."

We headed outside into the cool night air.

"Wow! A motorbike?"

He handed me a helmet. "I like to go fast."

Thank God for the darkness; I could feel my cheeks turn a deep shade of red.

I waited for him to get onto the bike before I slipped on the helmet and sat down behind him. He reached back, placed his hand on my lower back and pushed me right up against him.

"Put your arms around me and hold on tight," he yelled over the roaring engine.

I did as he told me. He revved the bike, then spun the back wheel on the gravel as we headed for the gates.

We rode past the forest, with just one headlight leading us away from Ella Moore.

I breathed in the scent of the pine trees, the cool air filling my lungs. It was great to be out of Ella Moore, great to be away from everyone.

I hung on tighter as he drove faster through the night. We rode for what seemed forever, yet the scenery never changed.

I felt the bike slowing down and I looked over his shoulder.

A quaint little diner sat in the middle of nowhere. The dusty carpark was empty. Nathaniel switched off the engine, took off his helmet and shook his hair into place.

I got off the bike and placed my helmet on the seat.

"Was that your first time?" he asked, smirking.

"On a bike? Yeah, how did you know?"

"I think you may have cracked a few of my ribs." He laughed.

"Oh I'm so sorry."

"I'm kidding, come on." Nathaniel took my hand in his and we walked into the diner.

"Hey Nate, haven't see you around here for a long time. Where you been, handsome?"

The pretty raven-haired waitress ran her hand along the side of his face.

He pulled back and smiled.

"Sara, this is Harper."

Oh great, he knew her name.

She winked at him and nodded her head. "I've got just the table for you two," she said, showing us to the back of the room.

I thought it was odd that she would sit us all the way back here when there was no one else in the restaurant.

We followed her over to a darkened booth.

"Ah, just the way I like it," Nathaniel said as we sat down opposite each other.

"What can I get you?" Sara asked.

"Burger with the lot and a scotch," he told her.

I looked at him blankly. Was he really going to order alcohol? Clearly, the answer was yes.

"Fries and a soda please."

She gave Nate a wink before walking away.

"Geez, someone wants you bad." I laughed.

"Who? Sara?"

"Oh come on Nathaniel, she is all over you."

"Sara and I have history."

Oh great. Why did I even bring it up?

"Oh." I blushed. Not wanting to know.

"It gets lonely at Ella Moore."

"Nathaniel, please," I stopped him. "I don't want to hear it."

"I like you, Harper, I want you to know that."

"Are you always like this?" I asked.

"Like what?"

"Forward, flirtatious?"

"Only with you."

"That's a lie."

I looked up to find Sara back at our table with our drinks. Was it getting hot in here?

"Sara, please, don't give away all my dirty little secrets." He smiled at her.

I was getting hot, too hot. It was as if someone turned up the heat one hundred degrees.

Before Sara had a chance to put my drink down, I snatched it out of her hand and placed the straw between my lips.

Nathaniel was watching me. He didn't once take his eyes from mine. "That will be all, Sara," he said. His voice was low.

Still sculling my soda, I watched her walk away.

I couldn't get enough of the ice-cold drink. I hadn't realized how thirsty I actually was and how good it tasted through the waxy straw.

"That's the way," Nathaniel purred. "Drink it all up."

"What?" I asked as I placed my glass down.

"You are so trustworthy to come here, alone with me. To think that Ms Moore would let you of all people leave the sacred grounds of Ella Moore."

"What?"

Why did my head feel heavy all of a sudden?

"To come here with a complete stranger." Nathaniel's eyes turned dark, almost black as he held my gaze.

I felt like I couldn't blink. I couldn't tear my eyes away from his.

I reached for my drink and took another long sip, draining the liquid completely. Why was I so thirsty?

"That's a girl, drink it all up."

I shook my head at him. "What are you talking about?"

Why was he going in and out of focus?

"Are you feeling okay, Harper? A little light-headed, perhaps?" He grinned.

"What?" I couldn't focus. Why was he slurring his words?

I looked down at his drink. He hadn't even touched it.

"My, my, this is going to be easier than I thought."

"Easier? What are you saying? Is it getting smoky in here? Can you smell smoke?" I coughed a little.

Something was wrong. I didn't feel right.

"Hmm, yeah I can," he replied casually. "We should get out of here." He slowly got out of his seat and pulled me to my feet.

I swayed a little as I tried to focus on my surroundings. The room was filling fast with smoke.

"Stay close to me," he whispered in my ear as he let go of my hand.

I nodded my heavy head, trying not to inhale the smoke that surrounded the room.

"Nathaniel?" I coughed as the smoke entered my lungs.

"Right this way, Harper."

I had lost sight of him; the smoke was too thick. His voice seemed distant, and I couldn't take another step.

"Nathaniel?" I screamed.

Panic had set in and I couldn't see him anywhere. A loud cracking sound came from above. I turned around just as a large beam fell from the ceiling above. It came down fast, whacking me on the back of my head.

I fell to the floor with the most excruciating pain ripping though my brain. I thought I could hear the sound of a motorbike in the distance as I closed my eyes, surrounding myself in darkness.

Chapter 15

"Harper, can you hear me?"

I couldn't find the words to speak. My head was throbbing.

"Harper, open your eyes, look at me. Goddamnit; don't let him win, not now that you see me. Open your eyes, Harper, look at me."

I couldn't open them. What was wrong with me?

"Harper, please, please open your eyes and look at me."

With all my effort, I forced my eyes open. "William?" my voice croaked.

There on the dirt and gravel, William was holding me in his arms. He pulled me closer to him and held me tight.

"What are you doing here?" I asked.

"I'm here now," he said, ignoring my question. "He's not going to hurt you anymore."

"Hurt me? Who's not going to hurt me? What are you talking about?"

My head was pounding; I had no idea what was going on. William sat me back slowly.

"Where are we?" I looked at the forest that surrounded us, illuminated by car headlights. "What are we doing on the ground?"

"Does anything hurt?" He asked.

"Just my head. What happened?"

William swallowed hard. "Nathaniel had an accident, you got flung from the bike."

"I did?" I couldn't remember. "Where's Nathaniel? Is he hurt?"

"He's fine," he seethed.

"I want to go back to Ella Moore."

William frowned, his eyes full of concern as he gently pulled me up off the ground and into his arms.

"Thank you." I smiled up at him.

"Can I ask you something, Harper?" he began as he opened the car door for me.

"Of course."

William turned me to face me. "What were you thinking leaving Ella Moore with him?"

I picked up annoyance in his voice. Or was it jealousy?

I looked past his red lips and into his blue eyes.

"I'm sorry, William."

"You're sorry? You would have been sorry this time if I hadn't shown up."

"What is that supposed to mean?"

"Nothing. Harper, you need to be more careful. Come on, let's get you home."

He placed his hand on my lower back and helped me into the car, closed the door and got in the driver's side.

"Wow, this is a pretty fancy car. What is it?"

"This here is a 1948 Buick Eight, Roadmaster, 320 76c convertible," he stated proudly. "Clearly it isn't mine. It belongs to Ms Moore, she lets me look after it and in return I can borrow it from time to time."

"It's beautiful."

As I looked around the interior, I rubbed my head.

"Are you okay?" he asked, looking me over.

"A little sore and shaken. Would you mind if I sit next to you?"

I noticed his body tense as he gripped the steering wheel tighter. He was staring straight ahead.

"William?"

He turned to face me.

"What? No, of course you can, slide on over." He smiled.

I slid across the red leather seat and sat as close to him as possible.

"I think I should take you to the infirmary when we get back."

Infirmary?

"I'll be okay," I said, ignoring his odd choice of word for hospital.

William looked straight ahead, his eyes fixed on the dark road stretching out before us. He gripped the wheel tighter as he pulled the car back on the road.

I sat there next to him, his scent of pine needles wafting through the air.

"What happened?" I asked.

"What do you mean?"

"Out here. What was I doing out here? I can't remember."

"Nate had an accident, you got flung from the bike."

"He left me behind?" I asked, confused.

"He left you for dead."

I shuddered at his choice of words.

The more I sat there in the quiet car, the more I thought about what had just happened. A shiver ran down my spine as I glanced over at William.

"Did he ask you to come and get me?"

"What?"

"Nathaniel, did he tell you where I was?"

"I haven't seen Nathaniel, Willow told me you were going out with him tonight."

I was so confused that it made my head ache even more. I rubbed my temples, trying to ease my headache.

"Harper?"

"I don't remember seeing Willow, and I don't remember being on a bike with Nathaniel."

"Harper?"

"Why can't I remember anything?"

William pulled the car over to the side of the road and switched off the engine. He turned to face me, taking my hand in his.

"Harper, something has happened. There was an accident at Ella Moore. It involves Willow."

"What accident?"

"She's gone, Harper."

"Is she okay?"

I wasn't understanding the conversation.

He shook his head no.

"She's—" I swallowed hard. "Dead?"

"I'm sorry, Harper, it was a terrible accident."

"What do you mean?" I asked as I rubbed the back of my head. I could feel a lump the size of a golf ball.

"About half an hour after Willow spoke to me, I went to see Ms Moore to see if I could borrow the car. While I was talking to her, there was a blood-curdling scream. We ran out to see what was going on, only to find Willow lying in a twisted heap at the bottom of the stairs. Nobody witnessed what happened."

I sat frozen, staring at him with my mouth wide open. I think I actually forgot how to blink.

"I don't..." I began.

"She's gone, Harper, I'm sorry. I should get you back to Ella Moore. You will be safe there. You are in shock, and you should see a nurse, just to be sure."

Safe? What did he mean by safe?

I nodded my head as William started the car and headed back to Ella Moore.

Willow was gone... forever. My stomach twisted.

I looked straight ahead at the low mist that had rolled in from nowhere. I closed my burning eyes and thought back to the night of the dance. Things had certainly gotten worse since I had arrived at Ella Moore.

Instantly, flashes of the accident played in my mind. I tried hard to see everything that happened.

I opened my eyes and sat bolt upright.

"It was a man," I yelled out.

William glanced my way. "Harper, are you okay?"

I slid as far away from him as possible, backing myself up against the door.

"Harper, you are starting to worry me."

"It was a man, I was right. He was tall, dressed all in black."

I wasn't sure if I was on the verge of a meltdown or a panic attack. My heart was racing.

William kept throwing odd looks my way. "Are you sure you are okay?"

"They told me it was a raccoon, a raccoon, can you believe that? And they call me crazy."

I felt the car speed up as I glanced over to William.

"You think I'm crazy too, right?" I laughed.

"No, Harper, I don't, I think you hit your head pretty hard though."

"There was someone out there the night of the accident, someone besides Ryan and me. When Ryan lost control of the car and it flipped, landing on its roof, I saw him." I watched William carefully for any sign of understanding.

His facial expression never changed.

"He was tall, kind of like your height, I didn't see his face, couldn't. All I saw was his boots." I glanced down at the floor to see what shoes he was wearing, I couldn't tell.

"Somebody must have stopped for help, that's all."

"No, no, there were no other cars on the road."

William made no response; he just gripped the steering wheel more tightly and pushed his foot further down on the accelerator.

We were speeding through the dark night; the trees outside the car blurred past us.

Why was he acting weird? Why didn't he believe me? I'd thought of all people William would understand.

Chapter 16

I sat listening to the sound of the engine humming and the tires pummelling over the ground outside. Nothing made sense, not Nathaniel, not William, not Willow's accident, not Ella Moore.

I sat watching William's blank expression as he focused on the road ahead.

"Why are you at Ella Moore?" I asked him.

He let out an uneasy laugh before looking my way. "What?"

"You? What's your story?"

"I, well, I don't like to talk about it."

I didn't believe him. "Can't be that bad."

He shook his head.

"What's up with you and Brittney?" I asked suddenly.

"Brittney? Why would anything be up with her? That's a bit of an odd question," he said as he glanced over at me then back to the road.

"I don't think so," I replied coolly.

"Nothing is going on between me and Brittney, why don't you see that?"

"It was just a question, William." I turned and looked out my window.

We sat in silence for what seemed like forever as we drove back to Ella Moore. I couldn't have been happier when I saw the headlights shine on the imposing iron gates.

William stopped the car at the bottom of the stone steps and got out.

I was in no mood to wait for him to open my door, so I got out and slammed it shut hard.

William came around and stood so close to me that my back was pinned up against the cool car.

"Have I upset you?" He whispered as he ran his thumb over my cheek.

"No."

"I think I have. I know how to make it up to you." He smiled, melting me.

I swallowed. "You do?"

"Can I meet you in your room? I'll go put the car in the garage and I'll come up, okay?"

Speechless, I nodded my head. I stood for a moment, shocked. I waited for William to get in the car and drive off before I went inside, raced up the stairs and into my room.

I sat on the edge of the bed trying to piece the night together, but my mind was blank.

I reached over and switched on my bedside lamp before going over and turning off the main lights.

There was a soft knock at the door. My heart was racing as I opened it.

"Hi." William smiled.

"Hi," I replied bashfully.

"Can I come in?" he drawled.

I loved the way his messy hair fell across his forehead and the way he spoke with his eyes.

"Of course," I stepped away from the door.

He entered the room, closing and locking the door behind him.

"How are you feeling? Your head, your thoughts, Willow?" he asked, moving towards me.

I didn't want to think about Willow right now.

"I'm okay." I didn't move. I stood frozen to the spot.

William stopped right in front of me and reached up and touched the side of my face.

"You look so beautiful," he said.

I was confused: first Nathaniel, now William. It took the school dance for Ryan to almost kiss me; I'd been here two days and had both of them kiss me.

I smiled at the thought.

"William?"

"Shh." He leant forward and put his lips on mine.

I felt my body tingle. He reached up and placed his hand behind my head, entwining his fingers through my hair.

He pulled me in closer to him, so our bodies were touching; I ran my hands up his back. He pulled away suddenly.

"Come, let's sit." He smiled.

Sit? No, sitting was not an option right now.

William reached for my hand and led me over to the bed. I sat on the edge of it and looked up at him.

"I need you to do something for me," he began.

"Anything," I breathed.

He placed his hands on my shoulders and gently pushed me back, so he was half lying on top of me. He then ran his hands down my arms and entwined his fingers through mine.

"Let me try something, you have to lie very still, okay?" he whispered in my ear, pulling my arms up and holding my hands above my head.

I nodded my head, not knowing what he wanted to try.

"Lie very still," he whispered again.

Moving closer to me, he began kissing my neck; God it felt good.

I tried to remove my hands from his strong grip but failed miserably.

"Lie still," he spoke softly into my neck.

How could I lie still with him doing that to me? It wasn't fair, why wasn't I allowed to touch him?

"God you smell so good," he groaned as he sniffed my neck.

"Let go of my hands, William. Let me touch you too."

He sat up a little and looked into my eyes.

"After, just let me—"

"What?" I cut him off.

"You don't know how long I have waited to be this close to you, Harper." He let go of my hands, rolled off of me and fell against the pillow. I moved to lie next to him, propping myself up on my elbow.

What an odd thing to say.

"Are you okay?" I asked tentatively.

He looked over at me. "I can't talk about it now."

"Oh, okay."

"It's not you," he said.

"Of course." I lowered my eyes.

"I mean it, Harper, it's not you."

We lay there for a moment in silence.

"William, can I tell you something?"

He sat up and moved closer to me.

"Sure, Harper, anything."

"Well, I'm a little embarrassed to tell you this but…"

He reached for my hand and placed his fingers through mine.

"You can tell me anything, you don't need to be embarrassed." He smiled.

"It's just that when I'm with you I feel different."

"I know what you mean," he replied.

"I want to be honest with you; I like you, William, I really do."

"I like you too, Harper."

"It's just that when I am around you, I get feelings I have never felt before. I want you to hold me, touch me, kiss me. To be truly honest with you, I have never been with someone that makes me feel that way." I could feel my cheeks flush. I felt like I was in the sixth grade telling the cute boy I liked him.

"Am I your first?" he asked.

I looked at him, shocked. "I've never dated anyone before. Lame, I know."

"What about that Ryan guy?"

"Ryan was my best friend, my only friend, we grew up together."

"Did you ever kiss him?"

My insides turned to jelly with the way he was watching me.

"Once," I lied. "But believe me, it was only a G-rated kiss." I smiled.

William moved closer to me. "And mine?"

I looked into his eyes and my stomach knotted. My mouth went dry.

"Mmm, maybe PG thirteen," I gave him a coy smile.

"Well maybe I'll have to work on upping that," he said as he brought his face close to mine and kissed my lips.

I reached up and held his face in my hands. I knew not to touch his back or else he would stop kissing me again and I didn't want that. All I wanted was him.

He moved as close to me as possible. As soon as our bodies touched, I felt a bolt of electricity pass through mine.

God, I wanted him so bad.

I laced my fingers through his hair, pushing him closer to me.

"I want you, Harper, I need you," he said between kisses.

William ran his hand up my leg, kissing me passionately. I reached behind him and grabbed his t-shirt in both hands.

"Don't," he warned as he continued to kiss me.

"I wasn't going to…"

"Put your hands above your head."

"William,"

"Just do it."

I obeyed his odd request and put my hands above my head, William ran his hand up the side of my body, along my arm and grabbed both wrists in his strong hand.

He stopped kissing me and looked into my eyes, his face inches from mine.

"I'm sorry, Harper, it doesn't have to always be this way. It's just for now."

"I don't understand," I said.

"I'm not ready yet. I need to be in control. You can't touch me."

"I can't touch you?" I repeated.

"Not yet, I'm not ready."

"That's a little odd, isn't it? I mean it's okay for you to touch me, but I can't touch you?"

William closed his eyes. "Please don't make me explain it to you, not here, not like this," he said, opening his eyes once again.

His dark eye make-up made him look so sexy.

"Okay," I agreed.

"Thank you."

William sat up then got off the bed. He ran his hand through his hair.

"I have to go," he said suddenly.

I got off the bed and went to stand in front of him.

"Don't."

"I need to," he sighed, a look crossed his face as if he were in pain.

"Stay," I begged.

"I can't."

"Why?"

Before he could answer me, there was a knock at the door.

"Because that's why," he mumbled under his breath.

"Who would be here at this hour?" I asked, glancing over at the clock.

"Harper, are you in there?" a voice called from behind the door.

I looked at William, then back to the door.

"Nathaniel?" I called out.

"Yeah, it's me, can I come in?"

I looked back at William. He shook his head at me.

"Now, Nathaniel? It's eleven o'clock."

"Open the door, Harper," he ordered.

Ignoring him, I went over and unlocked the door. I glanced at William before opening it. His facial expression never changed. He had one look on his face and that look was angry.

I opened the door. "Nathaniel, what are you doing here?" I asked, frustrated, as I tried to block out William behind me.

He glanced over my shoulder then back to me. "How did I know that he would be in here with you?" he asked angrily as he pushed me away from the door.

"Nathaniel," William's voice was calm.

Nathaniel went over to William; they stood face to face, glaring at each other.

"Guys, please."

"Stay out of this, Harper, it's between Nathaniel and me," William retorted.

"Clearly you haven't told her," Nathaniel seethed.

"Not yet," William replied casually.

"When? When are you going to tell her?" Nathaniel yelled.

"I think it would be best if you leave, Nate. You are not wanted here."

"Oh I don't know about that William, the way Harper kissed me in the gazebo," he didn't finish.

With lighting speed, William had his hand around Nathaniel's throat.

"William, stop it!" I yelled.

"I can finish this right here, right now, Nathaniel."

"You don't have the guts, Will, or you would have done it all those years ago. You can't tarnish your perfect image."

"I think you should leave, Nathaniel, this time for good."

"You know I can't, you know I have one little job I have to take care of." Nathaniel glanced my way.

"You are too weak, Nathaniel, or your little job would have been done years ago."

"You kept getting in the way. You have fallen, William, face it."

A shiver ran down my spine. I had no idea what they were talking about. Somehow, though, I knew it was about me.

"I'm in love with her, Nathaniel, I have been for a very long time," William told him, as he let go of his neck.

"Aren't we all?" Nathaniel replied.

Whoa! Hold the phones! What in God's name is going on here?

I'd been here for two days and both the hottest guys here were in love with me?

When did my life become the centre of everyone's attention? Oh that's right, when I got off the cuckoo train at Ella Moore.

"I want you to leave, Nate," William ordered.

I noticed Nathaniel glance at the bed, at the rumpled sheets, then back to William. His face was red with anger.

"You didn't?" he hissed at William.

"It is none of your concern, Nathaniel."

"Oh yes it is, and you know it!"

I stood there in shock. I had absolutely no idea what the hell was going on.

"Just because you got it handed to you on a gold platter."

"Don't go there, Nathaniel," William warned. "You made your choice when you did what you did."

"I hate you," Nathaniel said, infuriated.

"You never used to, you made that decision too."

Nate turned to face me; his glare startled me. He strode over to me and took my face in his hands.

"Don't let him be your first, Harper, he will only be using you to get what he wants."

"Excuse me? Who are you to tell me whom my first time should be with?"

"Choose me, Harper," Nathaniel begged.

"Why would I? Do you forget you left me in the forest after we had an accident?" I frowned, trying hard to remember.

"I went to get help."

"No you didn't, you left me there."

"Harper, I am in love with you. Why can't you see that? Why won't you give yourself to me?"

I went over to the door and opened it. "I think you should leave, Nathaniel."

"I won't forget this, Harper. This isn't over," he spat.

"Just go," I said quietly.

He walked out of the room. I closed and locked the door behind him.

I looked over at William. He didn't say anything; he just motioned his head for me to go to him.

I walked slowly to him, thoughts running wild in my mind. I stopped within inches of his face and looked into his eyes.

He frowned at me, almost pained.

"What was that all about?" I asked.

"Come away with me."

"What?"

"Just you and me, I know a place. Ms Moore has a cottage in the woods; only she would know where we are."

"I'm not sure," I bit my bottom lip.

"Harper, please. I need to be alone with you and here—here obviously isn't safe."

"I..."

I didn't know what happened; everything moved so fast. One minute, I was standing talking to him, and the next I was lying on the bed with William half lying on top of me. He was kissing my neck, running his cool fingers down the side of my face.

"Please?" he moaned.

I gently pushed him off of me and sat up.

"If you think I'm going to have sex with you..."

"No, Harper," he cut me off. "That's not the reason. I want to be away from this place, away from Nathaniel."

I shivered at the way the word "Nathaniel" rolled off his tongue.

"Alone in a cabin out in the middle of nowhere is the best place for you to talk to me?" I asked, trying to comprehend everything.

"Yes," he sighed.

It was so hard to resist William; he was everything a girl could want.

"Okay." I smiled.

He sat up. "Thank you."

I nodded my head and watched him get off the bed; I got up and followed him over to the door.

"Seven tomorrow morning, be packed and ready," he told me as he gave me a quick kiss on the cheek before he turned to leave. He stopped to smile at me before he walked out, closing the door behind him.

Chapter 17

I locked my bedroom door and went to sit on the edge of the bed. I shook my head as I tried to replay the fight that just took place between William and Nathaniel. What were they on about?

I let out a big sigh. Why was this so complicated? I thought of William and the way he looked at me. The way he spoke with his eyes always turned my insides to jelly, and his touch. Just the thought of his hands on me sent tingles all over.

A knock at the door interrupted my thoughts on William. Hoping it was him, I raced over and threw it open.

"Nathaniel?" I was disappointed and shocked.

"Not who you were expecting?"

"I wasn't expecting anyone," I lied.

"Are you going to invite me in?"

"Why should I? Boys are not permitted in the girls' rooms."

He took a step closer to me, ran his hand down my arm and stopped at my wrist.

"Don't make me beg," he drawled.

"I'm sorry, Nathaniel, it's late and I don't want to talk to you."

"I came to apologize."

"For what part? The part where, you left me on the forest floor and didn't bother to come back? Or for what you said before to William?"

He looked over his shoulder to the corridor then back to me. "Please let me in, I don't want to talk to you like this," he said, letting go of my wrist.

Something in his eyes made me move back from the door. He entered the room, shutting it behind him. He slowly walked over and stopped close to me. I could feel his warm peppermint breath on my face.

"I panicked, when I saw you were unconscious, I panicked," he explained.

"But you didn't come back?"

Nathaniel placed his hand on the side of my face. "I sent William for you."

I was burning up inside. That's not what William had told me.

Nathaniel placed his lips gently on mine. "I'm sorry," he said as he kissed me.

I wanted to stop him, to tell him I didn't feel the same way. But I couldn't. Something lured me towards him.

I closed my eyes, and images of William's blue eyes and full red lips danced through my mind. I shut my eyes tighter, thinking I was kissing William; I pulled Nathaniel in closer to me.

"See? It is me you want?"

I opened my eyes and saw Nathaniel's green ones looking down at me.

"Nathaniel?" I blushed. "I'm sorry, I thought…" I shook my head.

He took my hand in his. What was going on? I could have sworn I was kissing William.

"It doesn't matter. Kiss me and imagine whoever you want to be kissing you," he whispered.

"Eww, Nathaniel, that is gross."

"What matters is that you are here with me now, right?"

I couldn't focus properly. My head felt heavy and it was extremely hot all of a sudden.

"I think you should leave, Nathaniel. I'm not feeling too good."

Ignoring me, he stepped closer; his hand found its way under my top and rested on my hip.

"I don't think you should be doing that," I told him firmly.

"Why? Am I driving you crazy? Getting you all hot and bothered?" he murmured seductively.

I closed my eyes as Nathaniel slid his hand to my lower back and pushed me closer to him.

As he nuzzled my neck, he placed his hand under my chin and lifted my face towards his. I opened my eyes and saw William standing before me.

"Kiss me." His voice lured me to his lips.

"William?"

"Yes, yes, it's me, William," he purred.

I pulled him closer to me and kissed him passionately. Unable to resist him, I lifted his t-shirt and ran my hands up his cool back.

"No," he warned.

I pulled back and looked into his eyes. They were jet black. Startled, I stumbled backwards.

"Nathaniel?" I asked confused, sure I was kissing William.

He blinked his eyes a couple of times and they returned to their natural green colour.

I straightened my t-shirt. "I think you should leave. Actually, I want you to leave."

"Please, please, don't make me go," he begged.

"I'm sorry, Nathaniel, but I get so confused when I'm around you."

"It's because of him, isn't it?"

"I just can't seem to think straight when I'm with you. Things aren't what they seem. I'm confused, I need you to leave."

"What is there to be confused about? You felt it, I know you did. I want you as much as you want me," he said.

I walked away from him and went over to the door and opened it. "You need to leave," I told him.

"It's William, isn't it? What does he offer you that I can't give you?" He walked over to me and stood close.

The heat returned to my body and my head felt heavy again. Why did this always happen when he stood this close to me?

"I need you to leave before…"

"Before what?" He smirked. "You lose total control and give yourself to me?"

"I'm sorry, what did you just say?" I shook my head.

"I know it is William you crave, you desire, but you can have me too."

"I don't know what you are talking about, Nathaniel."

He took a step closer to me, closing the gap. "Oh, I think you do," he replied softly. "I can smell him all over you. We can pretend, can't we?" he said as he sniffed my neck.

I pulled back and looked at him in shock.

"Get out," I told him.

He looked over at the bed, then back to me.

"Don't sleep with him, Harper, you'll be making a huge mistake. It will affect William more than you know."

With that said, he turned and left the room, closing the door behind him.

Chapter 18

The next morning rolled around more quickly than I had hoped. I climbed out of bed at six thirty and got organized to meet William in the foyer.

I grabbed my backpack and as I made my way out of the room, I found Brittney leaning on the wall next to my door.

"You are up nice and early, Harper," she said as she glanced down at the backpack in my hand. "Are you going somewhere?"

"Just going to the library to meet William," I lied to her, giving her a smug smile.

"Oh dear, haven't you heard? The only place William will be this weekend is in the infirmary."

"Infirmary?" I repeated.

"There was an accident in the early hours of the morning. Will decided to have a little drink or two before taking a walk around the first-floor ledge of the building. Heaven only knows what he was thinking. Unfortunately for him, he lost his footing and fell. Lucky for him, he didn't break anything—just a mangled hydrangea bush, a few scratches to his pretty face and some light bruising. So I guess you won't be meeting William in the library after all. Toodles." She waved as she turned and left me standing there in shock.

"Shit!"

I quickly went back into my room, threw my bag on the bed and went to find the map.

Where the hell was the hospital, sorry, infirmary?

I glanced over the map and found it on the second floor. I left my room and hurried upstairs to the hospital wing. I went over to the desk and asked for William.

Just as I rounded the corner, Ms Moore stepped out of a room.

"Harper, is everything all right?"

"Yes Ms Moore, I'm here to see William. I heard he was in an accident this morning?"

"Yes, he was," she said, watching me carefully.

"Is he okay?"

A smile crept across her stone-cold face. I wasn't even aware that she knew how to smile.

"Stay close to William, Harper, he is changing. He needs you." She patted my shoulder and walked off, leaving me standing there gaping like a fish out of water.

What did she mean he was changing?

I shook my head and kept on walking.

A doctor in a white coat came out of a room and stopped to face me. He looked eerily similar to Doctor Raphael.

"Are you Harper?" he asked.

I looked over his perfect features.

"William has been muttering 'Harper' since he was admitted. I'm just trying to track her down."

"Yes, I'm Harper, that's me."

"Right this way."

I followed behind his billowing white coat; the hospital was better than the one back home. You honestly wouldn't think it was inside a boarding school.

We stopped at a closed door with the number 22 on it. The doctor turned to face me.

"He's a little groggy from the painkillers, he may say some things that don't make sense. He's been asking for you, he's one lucky kid." He opened the door.

"Thank you." I smiled.

"Take all the time you need, Harper, I will tell the nurse at the front desk you want to be alone with him."

I nodded my head and entered the room. The doctor closed the door behind me.

I glanced over at the bed; William was lying on his back with his eyes closed. As I began to walk towards him, his eyes suddenly opened, startling me. I stopped walking.

He pulled himself up a little. "Harper?"

"Hi, William," I smiled as I moved to the side of the bed.

He reached for my hand. "Are you okay?" he asked.

"Me? What about you? What the hell happened? Brittney said you had been drinking."

William squeezed my and hand let out sigh. He looked tired.

"I'm sorry," I gently placed my hand on his bruised face. He reached up and put his free hand on mine, holding it there.

It became clear to me that this was no accident; someone did this to him.

He closed his eyes, enjoying the moment. It was hard to look at the expression of pain on his face. "William?" I whispered as I tried to fight back tears. "Who did this to you?"

He opened his eyes as I sat down in the chair beside his bed.

"I want you to know I wasn't drinking, Harper. I don't drink."

"It's okay," I reassured him.

"I don't know what happened," he frowned. "I was so happy you said yes to going to the cabin with me, I was on my way to see Ms Moore when …" He paused for a moment, collecting his thoughts. "Nathaniel."

I shuddered. "Nathaniel?" I repeated. "What does he have to do with any of this?"

"He was waiting for me in my room when I got back. We got into a fight. I don't know what happened or how I even ended up here."

How could that be possible? Nathaniel had been in my room very soon after William left.

"You look troubled, Harper," he said as he held out his hand for me to take.

Ignoring his outstretched hand, I stood up and kissed his lips. When I pulled back, he was looking at me in shock.

"What was that for?" he asked as I sat back down.

"Nathaniel couldn't have been in your room, William, because he was in mine."

He closed his eyes.

"Nothing happened William, I promise," I lied.

He opened his eyes and turned his head to look at me. "You kissed him," he began through clenched teeth. "Then you let that lying snake touch you." His eyes turned dark.

I felt panic wash over me. How did he know? "Wait, William, hear me out, please. I, I thought he was you," I said, confused.

"Harper, when are you going to listen to me? Nathaniel is not good for you. I think you should leave."

"What? Why?"

He closed his eyes again. "I'm tired, just go," he whispered.

I stood up and made my way over to the door. Before I left, I turned to look at William. He hadn't opened his eyes.

Oh no, what had I done?

Chapter 19

As I stood outside his room, my mind began racing. What had I done? How did he know about Nathaniel?

"Harper?"

I looked up to find Sid making her way over to me. I had never felt so relieved to see her.

"Hey." I gave her a weak smile.

"Have you got a minute to talk?" she asked softly.

"Sure."

"Let's walk," she motioned her head for us to move away from William's room.

Don't listen to her, Harper.

Was that William's voice?

"I need to tell you something about William and Nathaniel."

Walk away, Harper.

"Listen, Sid, the last time someone tried to tell me about those two, she ended up dead. I really don't think you should go down that path."

"But it's ..."

I shook my head at her. "For your own safety, keep it to yourself."

That's a good girl.

"I'm sorry Sid, I have to go." I said.

She nodded her head and walked off.

I hadn't taken more than four steps down the empty corridor when I heard my name being called again.

Oh no.

I stopped and turned around. Nathaniel was the last person I wanted to see, especially only a few doors from William's room.

I chose to ignore him and kept on walking. I didn't want to talk to him. He was the reason William didn't want to speak to me.

"Harper, wait, please?"

He caught up to my side and grabbed my elbow, preventing me from walking.

"Look at me, Harper," he ordered.

The magnetic pull I felt every time I was around him forced me to look into his eyes. He leant in close to my ear. "We need to talk," he whispered.

I felt his lips brush my ear as he spoke. My whole body tingled. He pulled back and looked into my eyes.

"I don't think it's a good idea for me to be alone with you, Nathaniel. I think what would be best is that you stay away from me," I said firmly.

A smooth laugh escaped from his lips, causing a shiver to run down my spine. "You and I both know that's not going to happen," he said as he began pulling me down the corridor.

"Where are we going?" I panicked.

"I don't understand why you don't want me like I want you," he said through tight lips. "I think it's time…"

"For you to let her go and stop all this, Nathaniel."

He stopped dragging me and we turned around.

"William," I breathed a sigh of relief.

He walked towards us slowly, closing the gap between us.

"It's okay, Harper, I'm here."

"I thought you were…" Nathaniel hissed.

"Was," William replied calmly, cutting him off.

Nathaniel tightened his grip on my arm, causing me to flinch.

"She's coming with me, William, and there is nothing you can do about it. You are too weak, I want this ended once and for all. If I can't have her, then neither can you."

"Give her to me, Nate."

I looked over William's shoulder and saw the doctor heading our way.

Nathaniel pushed me towards William. "This isn't over. She will be mine," he replied as he stormed off.

William pulled me into his arms and rested his chin on the top of my head.

"Are you okay?" he asked.

I stepped out of his embrace and looked at him.

"Am I okay?" I repeated. "What about you? You made me leave; I left you lying in a hospital bed not looking all that great. How is it possible that you are walking around as if nothing happened?"

"Harper, calm down."

"Nothing in this place makes sense. Not you, not Nathaniel, not even Willow dying. I want to go home. I don't want to be here." I desperately tried to fight back tears, but it was no use; they began to flow uncontrollably.

William reached out and pulled me into his arms again. "Don't cry, Harper," he soothed.

I buried my tear-soaked face into his hard chest. God, he smelt so good. I felt myself melt into him as he wrapped his arms around me.

"I'm sorry, it wasn't meant to be like this," he muttered into the top of my head before gently pushing me away from him.

I looked up at him with tears in my eyes. Why didn't I understand any of this?

"It's time, Harper, we have to do it, right now."

I wiped my eyes with the back of my hand. "Excuse me?" I felt my cheeks instantly turn red, with all sorts of outrageous thoughts running through my mind.

A cheeky little smile crept across William's red lips. "The trip I was going to take you on." His smile broadened.

"But I thought you didn't want to see me anymore. You told me to leave."

"I can't stay away from you, Harper, it hurts too much. Can we start again? Will you go to the cottage with me?"

I nodded my head. "Of course."

"I'll meet you in the lobby at noon, don't tell anyone where we are going. Only Ms Moore knows."

I smiled at him. I loved the way he was being so mysterious.

"Lobby at noon, don't tell anyone," I repeated.

"Great, I'll see you soon." He smiled and walked the other way.

I went back to my room and sat on the edge of the bed thinking about my little getaway with William.

Was I mad to go away with him?

Loud laughter and chatting snapped me back to reality. I looked at the clock. It was eleven fifty-five. Everyone was making their way down to the dining hall for lunch. William knew that; he knew if we left at noon, there would be no one around to see us leave. Clever.

I stood up and grabbed my backpack and opened the door slowly. It was quiet and empty. Everyone was gone.

I hurried out of my room and down the stairs to find William waiting by the front door.

"Ready to go?" He smiled.

"Ready."

I followed him outside. The same car he rescued me in was parked at the bottom of the stone steps.

As I got in, I glanced up to the second floor window and could have sworn someone was watching us, but I couldn't make out who.

"You okay?" William looked my way as he drove the car towards the gate.

As if by magic, they slowly opened.

I looked at him, then slid over to be closer to him. "I am now."

He placed his arm around my shoulder and held me close.

Chapter 20

The sky was clear as we drove out of Ella Moore. I turned to watch the heavy gates close behind us.

I sat there thinking about Ryan, about how simple my life was before the accident, before Ella Moore.

"Your mind is racing," William said suddenly.

"What?"

"You're thinking about Ryan."

"How?" I turned and looked at him.

William looked over at me. "I can make you forget," he said hesitantly. " I can take all the pain away, if you want me to."

I swallowed. "How?"

He removed his arm form my shoulder. "Take my hand," he said holding it out to me. "Trust me, okay?"

I slowly reached out my hand and took his in mine. A warm sensation followed by a slight buzzing feeling flowed through my body. I closed my eyes, letting the powerful feeling of peace and calm wash over me.

"What's happening to me?" I slurred, feeling quite tired all of a sudden. I closed my eyes.

"I'm making you forget, forget everything." William's voice seemed distant.

"Forget everything," I mumbled, unable to open my eyes.

"Sleep now." His voice floated towards me. "I will wake you when we get to the cabin."

I nodded my head and settled back in my seat.

I let the hum of the engine and the sound of William's fingers lightly drumming the steering wheel ease my mind. I fell asleep, peacefully. No dreams plagued my mind.

I didn't know how long I had been sleeping for when I heard William calling my name.

"Harper?"

I slowly opened my eyes.

"We are here."

Chapter 21

I looked outside my window to find darkness covering everything. William rolled the car to a stop a few feet from the cabin and switched off the engine.

We sat in dark silence, with the headlights illuminating the cabin's wooden frame.

William drummed his fingers on the steering wheel nervously; I stared straight ahead at the quaint log cabin and wondered what waited for me behind the door.

Out of the corner of my eye, I saw him turn to me.

"Shall we?" he asked.

I turned to face him. I was nervous.

"Okay." I nodded.

"Wait there." He smiled as he got out of the car and came over to my side.

As he opened the door, he gave me another smile. "Harper."

"Thank you." I smiled back as I slid out of my seat.

We grabbed our bags, headed for the cabin and went inside.

"I can't believe how dark it has gotten. How long were we driving for?" I asked.

"A few hours. I'll go start the fire," he said.

I nodded my head. The way he looked at me before he turned and attended to the fire sent butterflies in my stomach flying.

I went and placed my bag by the coat stand, trying to calm my nerves.

"Ah, perfect," he said as he stood up.

William had the fire blazing within seconds, with a soft orange glow creating dancing shadows around us. We stood there, staring at each other from across the room.

"Harper." He gave me a sexy come-hither look that made me melt.

I walked over to him slowly, taking in every inch of him. The way he stood, his head cocked slightly to the left, the way his lips were partially opened, the way his chest moved up and down as he breathed, and the way he was consuming me with those blue eyes.

As I took my final step towards him, he reached out, rested his hands on my hips and pulled me in close to him. I placed my hands on his upper arms.

William locked his eyes on mine.

"You're not wearing any eye make-up," I said.

"Kiss me," he murmured, placing his lips on mine.

I pulled him in closer to me, kissing him, devouring him. I reached behind him and grabbed a handful of his tight navy t-shirt. William pulled my hand away.

"Wait," he urged between kisses.

I pulled back and searched his face for an answer.

"What is it?" I asked.

"Come, let's sit." William took my hand in his and led me over to the sofa.

We sat down, facing each other.

William reached into his pocket and pulled out a little black box. "Happy early eighteenth birthday, Harper," he smiled.

"It isn't my birthday yet."

"I know. Open it."

I took the little box out of his hand and gently pulled the lid off. A beautiful white gold infinity ring lay on a white satin pillow. I gingerly picked up the ring. Engraved on the inside were the words *Love forever - William.*

"Oh, William, it's beautiful," I said, slipping the ring on my finger.

A gorgeous smile crossed his luscious lips as he took the box out of my hand and placed it on the table. The orange glow from the fire made him look even sexier and more desirable than ever.

He pushed me back gently so that I was lying up against the oversized pillow, then moved to be half lying on top of me. My heart smashed against my chest and my breathing quickened.

His body felt heavy against mine as he leant forward and began to kiss me. I gently kissed him back.

He pulled away and looked at me. "Harper, is something wrong?"

"No," I said, biting my bottom lip.

"Are you sure? Am I moving too fast?"

I felt my cheeks flush instantly. Why was he so hot?

"I'm sorry, William, but I need to tell you something."

He propped himself up on his elbow.

"What is it, Harper?"

I looked into his blue eyes. "It's about Nathaniel," I began nervously.

I felt his body stiffen.

"Choose me," William whispered so softly I barely heard him.

I shook my head. "What?"

A pained expression crossed his face. "Choose me over Nathaniel, please, Harper?"

"I, I wasn't…" He never let me finish what I was going to say.

"Nathaniel is no good for you, Harper, do you not see that? He has tried to kill you more than once."

A shiver ran down my spine. "Excuse me?" I looked at him, shocked. "What did you just say?"

William let out a deep sigh. "You almost drowned when you were three, got hit by a car at the age of ten, involved in a car rollover when you were seventeen, and then there was the diner incident."

"Diner?" I asked confused. "What diner?"

He ignored me. "Do you see what I am saying, Harper? Accident-prone? I think not. Nathaniel is the cause of everything I just mentioned. Did you know that?"

"Why would you say such a thing?"

William took my hand in his and moved closer to me.

"This is going to sound crazy, right? But you need to listen to me, you can't freak out. We are in the middle of nowhere; there isn't anywhere to run to. We are safe here, protected. Do you understand me?"

Suddenly, being alone with William didn't seem like such a good idea. What was I thinking coming all the way out here with a guy I didn't really know? I shuddered at the thought.

He let go of my hand and stood up. I sat up and watched him carefully.

What he did next took me by surprise. Still facing me, he took off his t-shirt, unveiling a toned muscular torso. I felt my breath catch in my throat.

Holy crap!

"I need to show you something," he said slowly, not taking his eyes off mine.

I think you have shown me already, I thought to myself.

"I need you to stay calm."

I think it's too late for that.

"Don't freak out, okay?"

I nodded my head. *I'm already freaked out at your hot body,* I wanted to yell at him.

Still facing me, he took a couple of steps backwards towards the fireplace. He was watching me a little too carefully – as if I was going to jump up and run out of the cabin screaming.

He turned slowly and placed his hands on the mantle and leant into it.

I glanced from his lower back up to his shoulder blades. I couldn't believe what I saw. The pain he must be in; no wonder why I wasn't allowed to touch his back.

I stood up and went over to him.

"William?"

He didn't move, didn't turn around.

"I'm changing, Harper."

What was that supposed to mean?

I slowly ran my hands up his back to just below his shoulder blades. His skin was cool even though he was shirtless and standing in front of the fire.

My mouth went dry. "What are they? Did Nathaniel do that to you?"

At his shoulder blades were two long, deep scars that looked red, raw and bruised.

I reached up with my left hand and touched one of the marks. I felt his body tense at my touch. He turned around slowly, grabbing my wrist in his hand.

"Something is happening to me, Harper, I don't know why, but it's been since you came to Ella Moore."

He was breathing heavily, and his eyes had turned dark blue.

"What are you talking about? And what do you mean it's been ever since I came to Ella Moore?"

"Wings. Every angel has them." He smiled.

"What?" I asked, confused. What was he talking about?

William escorted me over to the sofa and we sat down facing each other. He reached for his t-shirt and slipped it on.

"You need to hear me out, okay? What I have to tell you will shock you, but you need to be aware and focus on everything I have to say, do you understand?" His piercing blue eyes had turned almost black and they were staring straight into mine.

What could be so life-changing that he has to demand my attention so intensely?

"Yes," I nodded.

William took my hands in his. "Don't be scared. I'm not going to hurt you."

Geez, I wish he would stop saying that.

"I have never felt so alive being with you." A tiny smile played on his lips. "Alive, I had forgotten what that felt like until now."

I shook my head slightly at him—I couldn't follow what he was on about. William moved closer to me.

"You make me feel so young again."

"What do you mean, William? Now you are starting to scare me."

He let out a deep sigh. "Just stay calm, I have to tell you a story."

I nodded my head.

"I was born in 1886 and died when I was eighteen in 1904. I have been this way for over one hundred years. God decided to give me another chance, this time as an immortal and as a guardian angel. I was sent to Earth to protect you, not fall in love with you." He stopped talking and just looked at me.

"Fall in love with me? Immortal? Guardian angel? God? I'm not understanding, William."

"Yes, Harper," he sighed. "I am a guardian angel sent to Earth to protect you, and yes, I am madly in love with you."

I pulled my hands from his and stood up. I paced back and forth in front of him.

"Why me?"

"Because of Nathaniel."

I stopped short and looked at him. Before I could say anything, he continued.

"When I became an angel, I was given the golden rule book. Rule one: never fall in love with a mortal, especially the mortal you are sent to protect. This was easy until I met you. I have been watching over you since the day you were born. When you were three and almost drowned, I saved you, when you got hit by that car when you were ten, I saved you. I slipped under the radar when you and Ryan became close; I couldn't handle it. I was falling in love with you by then, but I was stupid to think I could get you to fall in love with me. I longed for the way Ryan looked at you, the way he touched you, the way he made you feel. Because of this, I wasn't there for you when he had the car accident, the night of the dance."

"You caused the accident?"

"No, that wasn't me." He shook his head. "That was Nathaniel."

"Nathaniel? Is he one too?"

"Yes. It was stupid of me to leave you alone; it was the perfect opportunity for Nathaniel."

"But why? Why would he be so horrible to do something like that? What did Ryan have to do with anything? Actually what did I have to do with anything? What did we do that was so wrong?"

William reached for my hand and sat me down facing him. "It's not what you have done, Harper, it's what Nate has done. I was sent to protect you, I fell, Harper." He swallowed. "I fell in love with you. I wasn't there for you when you had the accident; I had separated myself from you. I'm sorry, I let you down, and he almost had you. It was you who was supposed to die, not Ryan."

I shook my head, trying desperately to understand.

"Why do you need to protect me?"

"This is where the story gets messy Harper, I hope you are ready."

Chapter 22

"What I have to tell you is quite disturbing, Harper. I need to know if you are ready for the truth."

I looked into William's eyes. They were mesmerizing. "Yes," I exhaled. "I am ready."

"Has your mother ever told you how you were conceived?"

"William! Yuck, no!"

"I don't mean the finer details, Harper."

"Well what do you mean? It's not something we sit around the dinner table and discuss. Eww."

"She never told you about the man she met in the bar?"

"Bar? My mother would never, ever set foot in a bar," I scoffed.

"Did you know she worked in one before she met Phil?"

"No."

"Then I guess she never told you who your real father is then?"

"Phil is my father. What are you talking about?"

William hung his head and sighed. "This is going to be harder than I thought. Your mother should have explained all this to you."

"Don't you back out now, William, you have to finish what you started. Who is my father then if it isn't Phil?"

William watched me carefully.

"It's Nathaniel."

"What? No that is sick! He is the same age as me, that makes no sense."

"I'm sorry, Harper, it's true," William said sorrowfully.

I shook my head. "No, no it can't be true."

"Nate is what they call a Nephilim. They would come down to Earth and seduce Earth women, taking on any look, any age they desired. One night while your mother was waitressing in a bar across town, a tall handsome man walked in and caught her attention. That man was Nathaniel; he wooed her with quotes from Shakespeare. His alluring good looks made it too easy for him to seduce her. She had no idea what he was. They drank expensive wine after her shift, and the entire time she was with him he forced her to forget about Phil."

"No, no." I shook my head in disbelief.

"They had sex, Harper, and not just everyday ordinary sex. It was dark, the work of the devil. It took only one night; the next day she woke up in a hotel room in an empty bed not knowing how she had got there or why. You were conceived that night."

A single tear rolled down my burning cheek. "Why would you say something as horrible as that, William? Phil is my father, not Nathaniel."

I sat for a moment, confused, with my thoughts so foggy I couldn't think straight.

William just sat there not saying anything, just giving me time to process his twisted and warped story.

"Oh my God! I kissed him, on the lips, my own father! I think I'm going to be sick!"

"Take a breath, Harper. Don't think of him that way."

I looked up into his eyes. Was he for real?

"The other day, after you left, he came to me, we kissed. I thought it was you."

"That's what he does, Harper, he manipulates you into thinking he is someone he is not."

"Why does he want me dead? Why do you have to protect me?"

"Nathaniel needs to destroy his Nephilim offspring. It was Doctor Raphael that mentioned Ella Moore to your mother. He told her what she told you—it's a school where you can get better, be with kids who are like you, Nephilim kids."

I looked at him dumbfounded as he repeated most of my mother's sales pitch on Ella Moore.

"Doctor Raphael?" I asked. I was trying to piece everything together.

"Yes, Archangel Raphael."

"Holy shit! I knew there was something odd about him. So my mother had no idea that she slept with Nathaniel that night?"

"None. If your mother was to meet Nate today, she would have no idea he was the one who slept with her."

"So she has no idea what he is, that I am the daughter of a, what did you call him?"

"Nephilim."

"Yes, that."

"Correct."

"So what is Ella Moore? Why did Doctor Raphael want me to go there? Is it like Xavier's Private Academy for Mutants? Does Wolverine, Storm or Magneto go there too?" I asked sarcastically.

"Harper, this is serious."

"Does Ms Moore know about all this?" I asked as I tried not to smile.

William gave me a look.

"Oh, is she an angel too?"

"Yes, she is a guardian angel like me. She watches over Ella Moore to keep everyone safe."

"Well how safe is it if Nathaniel is trying to kill me?"

"He used his evil ways to worm his way into Ella Moore, deceiving Ms Moore. He made her believe he was born from a Nephilim father and a mortal mother."

This was madness. None of what he was saying could be real. Could it?

"So you are not like him?"

"Like Nate?"

"Yeah."

William moved closer to me. "No, Harper, I am a guardian angel, I will never be like him."

I stopped and collected my thoughts. "Can I love you?" I asked carefully.

He chuckled at my question. "Can you love me?"

"I mean, I am in love with you, is that possible?" I shook my head.

"These feelings are new to me, Harper. Ever since you turned sixteen, I have had strong feelings for you. I tried to push them aside, I know it is wrong but..." He paused. "Ever since you came to Ella Moore things have been different for me. Seeing you every day, your scent drives me crazy. Knowing you can see me sends sensations flowing through my veins every day. I feel more protective of you, more than I should be feeling." William placed his hand on my cheek.

"To be able to touch you is incredible. I didn't ask for this life, I didn't ask to be your guardian, I didn't ask to fall in love with you. I'm changing, Harper, and I think it is all to do with you. Raphael is so angry with me."

"Wait, it was you he was arguing with outside my door that day at the hospital?"

"Yes."

"And it was you I saw at the cemetery?"

He nodded his head. Everything was flooding back to me. I looked into William's blue eyes.

"I got too close, I let you see me. The day of the funeral I couldn't believe you saw me, the real me. I had only ever appeared to you in shadow form, hiding my face, but I wanted you to see me so badly. That's why I appeared to you at the cemetery, that day you were at his grave."

"Ryan," I said, choking back tears.

"Sorry?"

"His name is Ryan." I swallowed, wiping my wet cheeks.

"Yes I'm sorry, Ryan." He looked down.

I was suddenly drawn to his blood-red lips; it was crazy how I was feeling. It should have been wrong, but I couldn't resist the desire to kiss him.

I just wanted to forget this crazy world William just introduced me to. I wanted everything to be normal, for William to be normal.

I leant forward and gently placed my lips on his.

"Are you sure?" he whispered softly.

"I've never been more sure." I smiled.

As our lips came together again, a small moan escaped his mouth, and he gently pushed me back.

"I want you so much," he said as he kissed my neck.

"I have to tell you something, William."

He sat up and looked at me. "Is everything okay?"

"No not really. I'm embarrassed to even tell you this."

"Hey, you can tell me anything."

I could feel my cheeks turn red. "It's just that I'm new to all this."

"All this, as in?" He was watching me intently.

"These feelings, I have never, well…"

"Oh, you mean to tell me you and Ryan never kissed?"

For the love of God, the humiliation was too much! I shook my head no.

"And you never, well you never got intimate?"

"No."

"Hey, there is nothing wrong with that. We can take it slow, I promise."

I got up and went to stand in front of the fire.

"Are you okay?" he asked.

I turned to face him. He was truly beautiful; it was obvious to me now that he was an angel.

"We need to figure this out," I said as I began to pace again.

He hung his head as if unable to look at me.

I stopped pacing and looked at him. "William?"

He looked up at me. "What is there to figure out? I have told you everything." He sighed.

"Us, Nathaniel, how do you think I am supposed to handle all of this? Do you think meeting angels is an everyday agenda for me?" I snapped.

He shook his head. "Please don't be angry with me, Harper."

"I'm sorry William, but you can't expect me to feel normal about all this."

"I know."

I took one look at the hurt and pain in his eyes and went over and knelt in front of him.

"I want to understand, William, but I don't normally believe in any of that stuff. Angels, devils, witches and vampires, they are all fictional characters to me."

"But I'm not fictional Harper, I am real."

"To a certain degree, yes." I shook my head; the thought of William being what he said he was just didn't seem real.

He reached down and took my face in his hands. Before I knew what had happened, I was lying on my back on the rug in front of the fire with William on top of me.

"Why don't we start again?" he asked. "Forget everything I told you, my feelings for you are stronger than I have ever felt before. Harper, I need to know if you feel the same way about me."

I looked into his eyes and smiled. How could I refuse him, no matter what he said he was?

"You just moved me two feet away from the sofa at lightning speed and you want me to forget everything you told me?" I batted my eyelids at him.

A smile crept over his lips. "Sorry, bad habit."

"Can you fly?" I asked him bluntly.

William laughed. "Can you just be quiet and kiss me?"

He leant down to me and gently placed his lips on mine.

He pulled back and took off his t-shirt and started kissing me again.

"Now you can touch me," he whispered into my neck as he kissed me softly.

My heart was racing as I placed my warm hands on his cool back and slowly ran them up to his shoulder blades.

As I felt the cuts under my fingers, he didn't flinch, he didn't stop kissing me.

It felt so good to be able to finally touch him and not be stopped. I pulled him closer to me, devouring every inch of him.

William ran his fingers along my chest as he kissed my ear.

"Your turn," he whispered, before continuing to kiss my neck.

"My turn?"

He rolled off me onto his back and placed his hands behind his head. My stomach was churning with the way he was watching me.

He smiled as he sat up. "Only if you are comfortable."

I smiled and shook my head at him as I crawled over to him slowly. I savoured every inch of his perfect naked torso.

He got on his knees and knelt in front of me. The orange glow from the fire danced wildly across his body as if enticing me to touch him. I stopped and knelt within inches of him.

William reached out slowly and lifted my t-shirt above my head. He ran his hands slowly down my naked arms, stopping to take my hands in his. He was watching me intently the whole time, not saying a word.

My mind was buzzing, and my body was tingling all over. I looked into William's eyes, and he nodded his head as he placed his hands just above the top of my jeans and pulled me closer to him.

He ran his hands up my arms then stopped at the straps of my bra. He leant forward and kissed my neck, then made his way down to my shoulder.

William stopped kissing me and looked up at me.

"Harper, are you okay?"

I shook my head no.

"What's up Harper, is it me? Am I moving too fast?"

I shook my head no again. I moved out of my kneeling position and sat with my legs crossed in front of him; he did the same.

He placed his fingers under my chin and pulled my face up so our eyes met. "You're not comfortable with this, are you?"

"I've never done anything like this before. I feel so awkward. I don't know what I'm supposed to do."

William took my hands in his. "You are doing fine Harper, it's only me so you don't need to feel like that, I'm not judging you but if you want me to stop, I will."

I nodded my head.

"You want me to stop?" he asked.

I searched his face.

"Okay, I'll stop," he said as he reached for my t-shirt and handed it to me.

"You're angry with me, William?"

He stood up. "No, Harper, I'm not angry with you. What I am, though, is hungry." He smiled as he stood up and walked out of the room.

Chapter 23

I slipped on my t-shirt and sat listening to cupboard doors slamming and pots banging around.

What had I done? Why was he so mad?

I stood up and took in a deep breath. Waffles. I could smell waffles. I shook my head and quietly walked into the kitchen.

I found William standing shirtless with his back to me at the hotplate.

I shivered as I looked at the two deep cuts on his shoulder blades. I couldn't even imagine how much pain he must be in.

You can do this, Harper. I tried to convince myself.

I slowly walked over to him and ran my hands up his back. He put the spatula down and gripped the sides of the counter.

The whole time, William didn't turn around. I took a step closer to him, my body almost touching his.

"It's not that I don't want you, William," I began as I kissed his shoulders. "It's just that I'm scared, scared of what you are, scared if I'm doing the right thing, scared because I've never had sex before." Saying it into his back was so much easier than saying it to his face.

I turned him around to face me and reached behind him to turn off the hotplate.

With lightning speed, he moved me across the kitchen and lifted me onto the counter he pushed my knees apart and moved closer, pulling me as close to him as possible.

My body tingled all over as new feelings ran through me. I couldn't believe how hot my body was feeling and how cool his body felt.

"Give in to me, Harper, I promise to do you no harm."

Thunder roared through the quiet night outside, as I nodded my head and placed my arms around his neck.

William picked me up off the counter, straddled me over his hips and carried me to the bedroom.

I smiled at him as he slipped off my t-shirt and tossed it to the floor. As he lay me down on the bed, a feeling of calm washed over me.

He knelt over me and placed his hands either side of my head and, leaning down to me, he kissed my lips.

I ran my hands up his strong arms as lightning lit up the night sky, filling the room with white light.

I grabbed onto his arms as he slowly lay his body down on mine.

"Are you okay with this?" he whispered in my ear.

I nodded my head.

"Close your eyes." He smiled.

I did as he asked and listened to the steady rain falling on the cabin roof. I let my body completely relax as he worked his hands over my body, down my stomach and stopping at the top of my jeans.

"Are you okay?" he asked, his body felt heavy against mine.

"Yes."

"Any time you want me to stop," he began as he kissed his way down my body, kissing my stomach and belly button.

I felt him fumbling with my jeans, then he pulled them off and undressed himself.

"Are you ready?" He asked getting back into position.

I nodded my head as we began moving together.

Suddenly my breath caught in my throat as William let out an almighty moan before collapsing on top of me. His breathing was coming in fast bursts; I ran my hands lightly over his back.

"Harper, that was amazing, you were amazing," he said as he nuzzled my neck before rolling off of me.

I lay on my back and pulled the cool sheet over my warm body. I couldn't believe I just had sex with William, my first time.

"Harper, come here," he murmured.

I snapped out of my thoughts and moved to lie on his chest.

"Are you okay?" he asked, running his hand down my arm.

"Yes," I exhaled. My body was tingling all over.

"I'm glad I was your first," he said as he kissed the top of my head.

"Me too," I mumbled.

"You tired?" he asked.

"A little," I slurred.

William was an angel and this was pure heaven on earth. I smiled to myself at the thought of what we just did.

William ran his hand over my hair; I felt my eyelids getting heavy. I closed my eyes and fell asleep naked in William's strong arms.

Chapter 24

As I opened my eyes, I was greeted by sunshine filling the room. I rolled over, grabbing the silk sheet in my hand. The bed was empty next to me, but a note and a white feather lay on the navy blue pillow.

I sat up, pulled the sheet over my naked body and reached for the note.

Good morning my love,

I hope you slept well after last night; it truly was one to remember.

I have just gone to get some supplies for breakfast; I'll see you soon.

W. xxx

I smiled; I was lying naked in bed, and the smell of William's aftershave wafted through the room. Snippets of last night flashed through my mind, causing my body to tingle all over.

A noise in the other room caught my attention. I got out of bed, wrapped the sheet around my body, grabbed the feather and tiptoed out into the kitchen. I found William at the refrigerator.

I crept over to him and ran the feather over his back to his neck. He jumped at the touch and spun around quickly, pushing me up against the counter.

"Harper, I'm sorry, I didn't hear you come in."

"I know." I smiled as I ran the feather down the side of his face.

He closed his eyes, enjoying the moment.

I gripped onto the sheet tighter as the overwhelming sensation to have him took over. He opened his eyes and pulled the sheet from my hand, allowing it to fall to the ground around our feet.

I stood there before him naked. He took the feather from my hand and let it fall to the floor as well. The look in his eyes was compelling. He bit his bottom lip as he picked me up and sat me on the counter.

He placed his hands on my thighs and then slowly ran them down to my knees. I watched him intently as he pushed them apart and moved in as close as he could, pulling me forward onto him.

I hurriedly took off his t-shirt as we kissed passionately, the heat in my body rising.

"Your skin feels so good," he said as he nuzzled my neck.

William took a step back, undid his jeans, stepped out of them and moved in close to me again. "I can't explain the feeling that is happening inside me, what you are doing to me, Harper, it is all new and feels so, so good."

It was all new to me, too.

I pushed him back a little and got down off the counter. I took his hand in mine and led him to the bedroom.

He scooped me up into his arms, carried me to the bed and put me down.

"Are you sure?" he asked as he lay down on top of me.

"I've never been more sure." I smiled at him.

"You were so great last night," he began.

"I was?"

"Yeah, you did everything right."

"I did?"

He pulled back and looked at me. "You seem a little unsure?"

"Well, I did tell you it was my first time," I blushed.

"You did great," he chuckled. "Trust me."

"Thank you."

William began kissing my neck. "You did so good, you made me feel so good. I haven't felt like that for a very long time."

I placed his hand on his chest and held him back.

"What is it?" he asked as he searched my face.

"You mean to tell me I wasn't your first?"

"You were my first this time."

"What is that supposed to mean?"

William moved off of me and looked at me, confused. "I have had other women, Harper, way before your time."

I shuddered at the thought. He moved closer to me and ran his hand over my body. I closed my eyes. God, it felt good.

"You are my first in a very long time, Harper. I wasn't even sure I remembered what it felt like, but you, you made it possible for me to feel lust, desire and pleasure again."

I nodded my head and pulled him to me. We kissed, then made love.

William rolled off of me, breathing heavily as he fell against the pillow. I rolled to face him and watched as his chest moved up and down with his heavy breathing.

"William?"

He opened his eyes and looked at me. "Are you okay Harper, I didn't hurt you, did I?"

"No, no, I'm fine. I just want you to know you were my first, my only."

"I know." He turned his head to me then pulled me into his strong arms and held me tight. We lay quietly for a while not talking, just enjoying being together.

I slipped out of his embrace and got out of bed.

"Where are you going?" he asked.

I turned to him and looked down at the way the sheet fell just below his belly button, his smooth chest and his naked body. I didn't answer him.

I felt my cheeks flush as I left him lying there and went into the bathroom.

I ran the hot water in the shower, filling the room with steam. As I stepped in, I let the hot water wash over me. I closed my eyes and thought about William.

I heard the bathroom door creak open.

"William?"

There was no answer.

"William, are you there?" I asked again as I rinsed the shampoo from my hair and turned off the water.

I pulled back the shower curtain, wrapping the white towel around my wet body. I walked into the bedroom and glanced over the empty bed.

"William?" I called, as I quickly got dressed.

There was still no answer. Where could he be? The cabin wasn't that big.

As I made my way out into the lounge room, I noticed my backpack zipper was open. I went over to it and saw a cream envelope sticking out of the top. I reached down and pulled it out.

"What have you got there?"

I spun around to find William standing there in only his black boxer briefs.

I felt my breath catch in my throat at how snugly they fit him.

"You okay?" He smirked.

It took me a moment to remove my eyes from the front of his boxers.

"Um, yes, I called you before, but you didn't answer," I stumbled.

"I was using the guest bathroom, taking a shower." He smiled devilishly.

The thought of his naked, muscular, wet body made me blush. "Oh."

He took a step towards me. "I thought of joining you in the shower, but I knew that I wouldn't be able to control myself."

He placed his hands on my hips and pulled me closer to him.

"You don't have to…" I began.

He raised an eyebrow.

"Control yourself," I told him as the feeling of wanting him began churning inside me again.

He looked into my eyes. "That's not what I got you up here for."

I placed my hand on his hip and ran my three fingers along the top of his boxers.

"You're teasing," he breathed.

"No, not teasing, wanting." I didn't take my eyes off his.

"Can I see the envelope in your hand?" he asked, ignoring what I just said.

I held it up for him to see. "What? This thing?"

"Yes, that thing."

I took two steps backwards away from him. "You want it, you come and get it," I teased.

"Oh really? You want to play games with me?" he said, moving slowly towards me.

I nodded my head and before I knew what was happening, William had pushed me against the wall and was kissing me passionately.

"God, you taste divine," he breathed into my mouth.

"Is this part of you?" I asked between kisses.

William pulled back and looked at me. "Part of me? What do you mean, Harper?"

"My heart is pounding, my blood is racing through my veins and this sensation that is flowing through my body is driving me crazy. I can't seem to get enough of you." I blushed.

William took my hand in his. "Why don't we go and sit down, see what this is all about." He waved the envelope in front of me, I hadn't even realized he'd taken it out of my hand.

I followed William over to the sofa and sat down next to him.

"It doesn't help, you know?" I began as I ran my hand up his thigh.

He turned to face me. His eyes were shining, and his breathing intensified.

"What doesn't help?" he questioned.

"That you sit here like this," I continued to run my fingers across the top of his boxers.

William drew in a breath as he closed his eyes.

"That's not fair, Harper," he sighed as he ran his hand down the side of my face.

"You're not stopping me." I smiled.

"I can't," he groaned.

I pulled my hand away and looked at him. "Can't? Have I done something wrong?"

"Oh no, no Harper, you've done everything right. But I need to stop for a little while, I'm changing, Harper, I just need to slow things down a little. Is that okay?"

"Of course."

Deflated, I flopped back against the pillows and nodded my head. "I understand."

But I didn't understand, any of it. What he told me he is, what I am, whether I did the right thing by having sex with him … twice. And what did he mean when he said he was changing?

"Now, shall we see what this is?" he asked, giving me a to-die-for smile as he tore open the envelope. Then something happened: the look on his face changed as he read the black calligraphy writing.

"Oh no, I forgot about the ball. Ms Moore told me about this the day you arrived at Ella Moore." He sighed as he shook his head.

"What is it?"

William looked up at me with fear in my eyes.

"This is not good," he said.

Chapter 25

"Can you please explain to me what's so bad about a ball, William? You make it sound as if it's going to be a world tragedy."

"It's the thirty-first of October, the day you were born."

"Do I want to hear this?" I asked.

"There's something you should know. My protection for you is growing weaker by the second."

"Because we had sex?" I asked, trying to make sense out of his dilemma.

"Well that didn't help matters, but it is more because you are almost eighteen."

"What? Why didn't you tell me this sooner, William?"

"That's not all."

"There's more?"

"It's worse. On the night of your birthday, there is something you need to do."

"Oh dear God, what?" I feared what his answer was going to be.

"If you want Nathaniel out of your life for good, you need to kill him."

"Excuse me, what?" My brain wasn't processing anything he was saying.

"Only you, his Nephilim offspring, can kill him."

"Could you have not put that in nicer terms?" I asked, slightly annoyed.

"There's one other thing,"

"Seriously?"

"There is a sacred dagger that you need to use to kill him."

"You're joking, right?"

He shook his head no.

I stopped and thought about everything William just told me. If finding out he was an angel and that Nate slept with my mother wasn't weird enough, this just topped the cake. How was I supposed to kill Nathaniel?

"Harper?"

"Do I have a choice?"

"No. He will not stop hurting you, hunting you until you are dead. Don't give into his good looks and charms. He is bad, Harper, very bad."

I sat, thinking about Nathaniel. Was he really that bad? Was he really trying to kill me? Did he really have sex with my mother?

"Yes, Harper, to everything."

I looked up at William.

"Trying to kill you, he is that bad and yes he had sex with your mother… sorry."

"How? Did you just read my mind?"

"Yes, I'm also the voice you have been hearing for all those years," he explained gently.

"Oh. Well I guess I should really start to control my thoughts," I said, embarrassed.

"No, I actually like the thoughts that go through your mind, especially since we have been at the cabin." He smirked. "Now back to Nathaniel."

"How do I do it?" I cut him off.

"With the ancient, sacred dagger. It holds many powers that only you can use. It is powerless if it is used by a mortal."

I looked at him, dumbfounded. "You're joking, right?"

He shook his head. "Unfortunately, I'm not."

"You know this is stupid, right?" I asked.

William didn't answer me.

"What do I have to do?" I sighed.

"You must kill him before the stroke of midnight. You need to drive the dagger straight into his heart."

"He has a heart?" I mocked.

"Harper…"

"Sorry, it's just that, well." I saw the look on his face. "Never mind."

"I know this sounds stupid and far-fetched."

"You think?"

"I need to know if you are okay with this."

"Oh yeah sure, I do this sort of thing all the time. No, I'm not okay with this. It's not a knitting class I'm joining for the first time; I have to kill someone."

"Okay, point taken. That was a silly question to ask." William dropped his head.

"Why do I have to kill him? Why can't I just move away? He has done me no harm."

"He has done you harm, Harper, many times. You are forgetting about all those accidents you had when you were younger."

"But recently he's done me no harm," I retorted.

"Come on Harper. Why are you trying to protect him? He is getting you on his side. He will feed you anything and you will believe him. He wants you, Harper, and if you give into him, you are his forever."

I shuddered at his words.

"But I don't want him, I want you."

"I know that, Harper, you've proved that to me twice." He smiled. "It upsets him to no end that you do not want him. He has turned this into a game and he will stop at nothing until he has you."

I began to really consider what William was saying. "I'm scared, William."

"And that's how he wants you. Vulnerable, frightened, wanting you to take his hand so he can make everything better."

I looked down at my nervously entwined fingers. This was certainly not normal.

"What if I get caught?"

"It's not like that. Ella Moore is a sacred place, on sacred grounds. Anything that happens there never leaves those gates."

I nodded my head.

"Why don't we change the subject?" He held up the envelope.

I nodded, even though that damn envelope was what got us on to the topic of me having to kill Nathaniel. I moved closer to him and snuggled against him.

"Okay, let's see," William began as he read the invitation. "A Moulin Rouge–themed masquerade ball, how interesting."

"Moulin Rouge?" I repeated. "Isn't that like corsets and fishnet stockings?" I asked.

William turned to face me. "My dear, you have nothing to worry about with a figure like yours. Just imagining you in that type of costume turns me on."

I punched him lightly on the arm. "Shut up!"

"Sorry," he laughed. "Just stating the obvious."

I snatched the invitation out of his hand, threw it behind me and grabbed his face.

"You make everything better," I told him as I brought my lips to his.

"You know we should really be getting back to Ella Moore," he said between kisses.

I pulled back and looked into his eyes. "Why? We just got here. I want to be alone with you, William."

"I know you do, I do too." He stood up and reached for his clothes. "But something doesn't feel right," he said as he got dressed.

"Like?"

"I think he's close."

"Who, Nate?"

"Yeah, you would be much safer at Ella Moore."

"Can you stay with me?"

"As in your room?" he asked.

"Yes, please, William, with everything you just told me, I'm scared to be alone."

"Okay. Let's get packed up and on the road."

Just as I stood up, there was a massive crashing sound outside.

"What was that?" I jumped.

Fear filled William's eyes. "Oh no," he breathed.

"Is it him?" I whispered, terrified.

"Get everything ready to leave, I'm going out there."

"William, no."

"Stay here. We leave as soon as I get back."

I nodded in reply as I watched him creep over to the front door and open it slowly. He turned back to face me before going outside and closing the door behind him.

I raced out of the room into the bedroom and threw everything into my backpack. Another crash outside made me jump.

I went back into the lounge room and peered through the lace curtains. A bright white light blinded me for a second; I blinked and saw Nathaniel punch William in the face.

William doubled back, holding his cheek.

"Why have you brought her here?" Nathaniel roared.

"To be alone with her. It's too late, Nate, Harper has already given herself to me."

"No!" Nathaniel shouted so loud the windows shook. "How could you?"

I watched in horror as he lunged at William. I couldn't take much more.

I paced around the lounge room, waiting for it to be over.

Suddenly the door flew open; William was standing there, breathing heavily. I raced over to him.

"Where's Nathaniel?" I said, panicked.

"He's gone, for now," he said, collapsing against me.

I helped him inside and sat him down on the sofa.

"You're cut but you're not bleeding," I said.

"We don't bleed the same way as you do," he told me.

"William, you look terrible," I sighed as I looked over his bruised face.

"He can throw quite a punch. I am no match for him, Harper, not anymore."

"I'm sorry," I spoke softly.

"I fought him off this time, but he is strong. Stronger than I've ever known him to be."

"Well if you can't beat him, how am I supposed to?"

William stood up and walked away from me, over to his bag. He came back and held out a shiny silver dagger. It was small and had blue topaz jewels on the handle. I looked at it and then looked back at William.

"That's it? That's the dagger I'm supposed to drive through Nathaniel's heart?" I asked, shocked.

William looked down at his hand. "Yeah, why?"

"Have you seen the size of Nathaniel? It's a bit small, isn't it?"

"It may be small, Harper, but the magic that lies within it is more powerful than you can imagine."

"Oh, okay."

Like that was going to make me feel better.

"Are you ready? I think we should get going." William held his hand out to me.

I didn't answer. I placed my hand in his. He pulled me up fast, causing me to crash into his body. I felt my heart beat faster as I looked into his eyes.

"Do we have to leave?"

"I don't want to leave, Harper, but we need to."

I reached up and ran my fingers through the back of his hair. "I want to stay," I whispered, my lips close to his.

"I promise you we will come back here again."

I took a step back and picked up my bag. "Okay."

"Don't be upset, Harper, please?"

"I'm not upset; you're right—we should get back."

He nodded his head, reached for my hand and led me outside.

I turned around and looked over the cabin. I closed my eyes and thought of our two intimate times together. Was that the whole reason William had brought me here?

"Harper, that's not the reason. I wanted to be alone with you without prying eyes."

I opened my eyes. "Sorry."

"It's time to go."

I smiled tenderly at him as I opened the car door.

Chapter 26

"Come along now Harper, we need to get going."

I nodded my head and got in the car. William spun the back tires furiously on the dirt track, leaving the cabin blanketed in a cloud of dust.

I looked over at him; his hands gripped the steering wheel tightly, his knuckles were red, raw and starting to bruise. His jaw was clenched tight and he stared straight ahead at the road stretched out before us.

"Are you okay?" I asked tentatively.

He glanced my way briefly and then back to the road. "Of course, babe, are you?"

I settled back in my seat and watched as the dark world outside whizzed by my window. "I'm a little scared."

"Of?"

"What you told me I have to do. I want to be with you, William."

"Once you kill Nathaniel, you and I can be together forever."

"Forever?" I turned to look at him.

"Yes, once Nate is out of both our lives, we will have nothing to worry about."

"Except the fact that I will grow old and you will never age?"

William turned to face me briefly before turning back to the road.

I raised my eyebrows at him waiting for a reply.

"I never thought of that."

"Well there's a thought for you now, William," I said bluntly.

"I'm not going to leave you, Harper, ever."

"Ah-huh."

"Can we not talk about that right now?" he asked.

"Sure." I looked back out my window.

"You know, if you like, tomorrow I can drive you into town to get your costume for the ball. Ms Moore normally organizes them but—"

"There's a town?" I cut him off.

"Yes, not a big one, but there is a drapery."

"A drapery," I interrupted him.

"Yes, and a butcher, a baker…"

"And a candlestick maker," I added.

William gave me a blank look. "I don't get it."

"Nothing, go on."

"Don't you think it will be fun shopping for costumes tomorrow?"

"Oh yeah, super."

William nodded his head and ended our conversation there. We drove through the night without another word spoken between us. Quite frankly, I was through talking anyway.

It seemed to take forever to get back to Ella Moore, and I was glad when the iron gates came into view. William rolled the car to a stop just at the bottom of the steps.

"Say, Harper, I've been thinking."

"Yes?"

"I think it may be best if you head up to your room alone."

"What? Why?"

"Well, Ms Moore doesn't really like us intermixing."

"Intermixing?" I repeated. "Are you serious right now, William? Don't you think you and I intermixed already? Twice."

I saw William's face blush under the soft glow of the coach lights.

"Harper…"

I got out of the car. "It's okay William, I get it. You did what you wanted to do with me, now you and I are done. Just stay away from me,

William, I can handle Nathaniel on my own." I slammed the car door and raced inside.

"Miss O'Connor?"

I stopped walking and looked up. "Ms Moore?"

"Where is William?"

"He's parking the car."

Her beady, cold eyes stared straight through me.

"Carry on." She turned and walked away.

I hurried up the stairs and into my room, closing the door behind me. I felt tears roll down my burning cheeks. Why was William being like this?

"Harper?" A voice called from behind the closed door.

Wiping away my fallen tears, I opened it quickly. "William?"

He pushed me back and locked the door behind me.

"You didn't mean it, did you? What you said when you got out of the car?" He stepped towards me slowly, watching me.

"No," I whispered.

When he reached me, he placed his hands on either side of my face. He brought his lips down to mine and began kissing me passionately. Melting into him, I reached up and ran my hands under his t-shirt, pulling him tightly towards me. He pushed me gently towards the bed.

"I couldn't stay away from you," he murmured as he lifted my t-shirt slowly above my head.

"I don't want you to, ever," I said as I lay down on the bed.

William smiled down at me as he took off his t-shirt. God, he was divine.

Our moment together was disrupted by an unexpected knock at the door.

I sat up fast. "Who could that be?" I whispered.

William glanced over at the clock. I put on my t-shirt as the knocking continued.

"I have to answer it," I spoke softly.

He nodded his head and gracefully moved to the other side of the room.

I opened the door. "Ms Moore?"

I was shocked and could feel my face turning bright red.

Without saying anything, she walked into the room, closing the door behind her.

"You can come out of the shadows, William, I know you are in here."

I watched, mortified, as William stepped out of the dark corner, still with his shirt off.

"Ms Moore," he began.

"Save it, William, I know what you and Harper have done."

"And so do I," a male voice spoke from behind me.

I spun around fast, hoping it wasn't Nathaniel.

"Doctor Raphael?"

What the hell was he doing here? And how did he get in the room? Was he here the whole time? I blushed at the thought.

"Just Raphael, Harper. Archangel Raphael."

I stood there, shocked.

"Yes, of course, sorry."

I didn't know whether to bow, shake his hand or call him sir.

"We need to talk, best you take a seat," he told me.

"I'm sorry, yes sit." I shook my head and went to sit down.

Ms Moore stood at the foot of the bed. I couldn't take my eyes off Raphael. He was more beautiful than I remembered.

"Your shirt, if you don't mind, William," Raphael said.

I watched as Raphael picked up the t-shirt from the floor and threw it at William. He waited for William to get dressed before he reached for the chair at my desk and sat down in front of me.

"Do you know what is going on, Harper?"

I looked at him, then to Ms Moore and then to William, who nodded his head slowly.

"Do you mean why you and Ms Moore are in my room?" I asked.

He shook his head and smiled slightly. "No, Harper, about you and William having sex."

I drew in a breath at his blunt words. Holy crap, did he just say that?

"Oh?"

"It's not good what you have done."

"It wasn't just me," I fought back.

"No, it was William too, I understand that. Do you know what this means for William?"

"No."

"He has turned his back on the gates of Heaven. Did he tell you that once you and he did what you did, he can no longer protect you? He is weak, and if Nathaniel comes within one foot of you, William can't do a thing about it."

I turned to look at William, who had hung his head to avoid looking at me.

"William, is that true?" I asked, remembering how we left the cabin so quickly.

Without turning to look at me, he nodded his head.

"So that's why you collapsed against me when you came back inside?"

Again he nodded, not saying anything.

"Was Nathaniel at the cabin?" Ms Moore spoke for the first time.

"Yes, he and William got into an almighty fight," I said as I looked at her stone-cold face.

Raphael got up and stepped in front of William. "Look at me," he ordered.

William looked up at him.

"I'm sorry," William said sadly.

"You're sorry?" Raphael repeated. "Do you know what you have done?"

"Yes, Raphael, I do. I broke the sacred rule, I had sex with a mortal."

"She is no mortal, William, she is a Nephilim offspring. That is worse. You know this makes you just as wicked as Nathaniel?" Raphael replied angrily.

"No! I will never be like him!" William cried as he glanced over at me.

A shiver ran down my spine when I saw the way he was watching me.

"I love her Raphael, I really love her. She was my first."

"Spare me, please, William, I can't help you now," Raphael replied.

With that, Ms Moore and Raphael left the room, closing the door behind them. William fell to his knees, holding his head in his hands. I raced over to him and knelt down in front of him.

Chapter 27

Cautiously, I reached out and gently ran my fingers through his hair.

"William?" I called softly.

He shook his head, disconsolate.

I pulled his hands away, to find he had been crying. Tears ran down his cheeks as he desperately tried to avoid meeting my eyes.

"Look at me, William."

He gave in and slowly raised his tear-filled eyes.

"It's okay," I said soothingly.

He shook his head. "No, no it isn't. It's really bad," he said as he wiped his tears away with the back of his hand.

"I don't care what Ms Moore or Raphael have to say about us. I want to be with you; I don't care what you are—that's not going to stop me loving you. My life is messed up anyway, my best friend is dead, my father is a Nephilim, Willow is gone, and my mother put me in this place. How much more messed up do you think things can get?"

William gave me a look.

"What?" I asked.

"Your mother knows, everything. I didn't want to tell you, I wanted you to hold on to the fact that you thought..."

"Wait. What? My mother knows what?" I shook my head.

"That is why you are here at Ella Moore. She knows it is a safe haven for you, she knows about the voices, she knows that the 'shadow man' is me, she knows that Nathaniel wants to kill you and she knows that he is your father."

"But I thought..."

"Forget about what I told you."

"You lied to me?"

"I wanted to protect you."

"From whom? My mother? This school? Nathaniel?"

"From me."

"From you? Why?"

"Because I fell in love with you. I am not human, Harper."

"And I told you I don't care, what you are saying is that I'm kind of not human either," I cried.

Another knock at the door stopped our conversation. I got up off the floor to answer the door.

William grabbed my ankle. "Don't."

"William, let go," I said as I tried to pull my ankle free.

"Please?" He begged. "Stay, I need you."

"What are you talking about?" An uneasy laugh escaped my lips.

The knocking continued. I broke free of his hold and stumbled towards the door.

I looked back at William, who had now stood up.

When I opened the door, Nathaniel pushed past me, slamming the door behind him. I shivered at the look of hatred in his eyes.

I wished I had listened to William and hadn't opened the door.

"You sick, sick, bastard!" he bellowed in William's face.

"What, Nathaniel?"

"Don't you 'what' me, I can't believe what you have done," Nathaniel yelled.

"We have already battled this one out at the cabin, Nate."

"And I've had time to process what you did."

"And? I can't take it back now, Nate." William replied coolly.

Nathaniel placed his hands on William's chest and pushed him backwards.

"I wouldn't do that if I were you." William warned him.

I stood there, frozen to the spot, with my heart beating fast.

"I want you to leave, Nathaniel," William said firmly.

In one swift move, Nathaniel punched William in the face. The blow was so powerful it sent William flying across the room, where he landed in a heap on the floor.

"William!" I screamed as he lay limply.

Nathaniel marched over to him and kicked his foot.

"Get up!" he yelled.

William didn't move. My hand went to my mouth. I felt as if I was going to be sick.

"Goddamn you, William!" He roared, as he began kicking him.

I raced over to Nathaniel and grabbed his arm. "Stop it, Nathaniel, please stop it."

He turned to me roughly with a look of hate in his eyes.

"Don't… you… touch… me," he retorted through tight lips.

I let go of him fast; there still was no movement from William.

"I don't understand. How did you get into Ella Moore if you are so wicked? It's supposed to be a safe place," I yelled at him.

Nathanial took a step towards me. "No place is safe, babe," he purred.

A shiver ran down my spine. I wanted to kill him right then and there. How could someone so beautiful be so evil?

Chapter 28

"What have you done to him?" I cried.

"Him?" Nate threw a glance over at William. "Don't worry about him, he knew what was going to become of him if he had sex with you. He played with fire."

I was terrified by the way Nate was watching me.

"What do you want from me, Nate?" My voice shook as tears began to flow down my flushed cheeks.

He stepped closer to me; I could feel his warm breath on my face.

"You," he whispered. "It has always been you."

A shiver ran down my spine.

"I don't..."

"The ball is in two nights. I want you to go with me."

"What makes you think I would do that?" I replied tersely.

Nate leant in closer to me, our faces were almost touching. "Because I am telling you to."

"But I'm going with William," I said. I could hear my voice wavering.

He ran his cool fingers down the side of my face. "Mmm... I can't see William being in any shape to take you anywhere; I'll make sure of that," he hissed.

"I want you to leave."

I glanced over at William, who was still lying motionless on the floor.

"Promise me?" he spoke.

I sighed. "Fine, Nathaniel, whatever. I'll go with you if that's what you want."

"No, no. You won't be going with me, you'll have to find me."

Leaving me with those mysterious words, he walked out the door and closed it behind him.

I shook my head and let out a deep sigh before I raced over and dropped to the floor next to William.

I leant down close to his face. "I'm going to get help, I'll be right back," I told him as I stood up.

"There's no need."

I turned around fast to find Raphael standing behind me.

"Oh I'm sorry, I didn't hear you come in," I stumbled.

He stepped around me and knelt down by William. He placed his hand over William's face, then looked up at me.

"Do you know what's happening to him, Harper?"

I shook my head; with the way he was looking at me, I didn't really want to know.

"He is changing. He doesn't have much longer."

"You mean he is dying?" I panicked.

"No, not dying, he is becoming mortal. I don't know how much longer he can protect you, Harper."

"Mortal? I don't understand. If he becomes mortal, how old will he be?"

Visions of William ageing rapidly before my eyes flashed through my mind.

"Eighteen, just like when he died. I need to get him to the infirmary where he can get some rest and be watched over. Clearly, Nate has it in for him, so I don't think leaving him alone is such a great idea. Go to the ball, be on your guard, do what it is you need to do. William may not be well enough or strong enough to be there for you."

I nodded my head as Raphael scooped William up into his strong arms.

"Don't forget, Harper, you have the ability to kill Nate. Also, remember you have until the stroke of midnight. Do we have an understanding?"

"Sure," I replied, but not really understanding anything he'd just said.

To my surprise, he didn't exit through the door. He evaporated into a cloud of thin, white mist with William still cradled in his arms.

I fell to the floor with my face in my hands. "Why is this happening to me? None of this can be real. If my mother knows all of this, why didn't she tell me?" I asked out loud.

"Your mother knows, Harper, your father too."

I looked up fast.

All of a sudden Nathaniel had reappeared in the room.

He reached out his hand to me as I looked up at him. I held out my hand and he pulled me up into his strong arms and held me tight. I melted into his chest as he ran his hand over my hair.

"I can make it all go away, Harper. She was beautiful, your mother, I was her protector, but I fell for her, not like William has fallen for you. It was more sinister—it was lust, not love."

I pulled back and looked into his green eyes.

"I had to have her, so I changed myself to look older," he continued.

"I don't want to hear this," I told him.

"Oh, but it is best if you do, so you can understand what you are."

"No thank you, I'd rather not know."

"Your father, Phil, knows, that's why he had no say in sending you here."

"But why?"

"There are others here, others like you. Born from Nephilim fathers."

I took a step back from him. "You're sick, you know that?"

He nodded his head. "When I was given this life, I had no idea it was going to be like this. I was good, Harper, you have to believe me, but then something changed inside me. I wanted my life back, to touch, to feel. That's when I fell for your mother; her skin was perfect, her hair smelt like strawberries, and the way she walked and laughed was utterly amazing."

"You're making me feel sick, Nathaniel, I need you to stop."

"When you were born, it didn't seem real, I needed you to die," he continued, not listening to me.

"Oh, that's charming,"

"You and me, we have a connection, my blood runs through your veins."

"I want you to leave," I said to him.

"Harper…"

"Get out, now," I ordered.

He hung his head and turned to go.

I waited for the door to close behind him before I fell on the bed, almost too exhausted to sleep.

Chapter 29

I was awoken from a dreamless sleep by loud knocking at my door. I sat up and stretched.

"Harper, are you in there?"

"Sid?" I called out.

"Yeah, open up."

I got out of bed and opened the door.

"Hey, what's up?" I asked her.

"You are half an hour late for class, that's what's up. I was sent to see if you were still alive."

"Of course I'm still alive," I scoffed at her.

"Get dressed, I need to get you back to class." She turned her back to me.

I shook my head at her weirdness and quickly changed into my jeans and t-shirt and slipped on my Converse hi-tops.

"Ready?" she called over her shoulder, not turning around.

"Yeah, I'm ready."

Following Sid down to the English room, I thought about what lay ahead of me and shivered as we walked into class.

"Ah, Miss O'Connor, good to see you made it to class, take your seat."

"Sorry," I mumbled as I sat at a desk at the back of the classroom.

I looked around the room as the teacher continued his speech on Shakespeare. I slumped back in my chair. I couldn't concentrate. I didn't care about Shakespeare's weird ways of writing.

"The guy is a freak," I mumbled to myself.

"Aren't we all?" a voice whispered in my ear.

I turned around to find Nathaniel had somehow made his way into class unnoticed and sat down in the empty seat next to me.

How is it he doesn't get humiliated in front of the whole class? I wondered.

He looked at me and smiled. I looked back at the teacher.

"I don't want to talk to you," I told him.

"Oh come now, Harper, don't be like that."

"Do you two need to be separated?" the teacher asked with his back to the class.

We stopped talking. The lesson seemed to drag on forever. As soon as the lunch bell sounded, everyone jumped out of their seats, including me.

"Hey, where are you going?" Nathaniel grabbed my wrist to stop me from walking away.

I turned to face him as he tightened his grip. "Let go, you're hurting me." I winced.

He stepped in closer to me and ran his hand down the side of my face. "Mmm sheer beauty, just like your mother. And just like your mother the lust and desire to have you is taking over me."

"You are sick," I said as I tried to pull my wrist free from his tight hold. "Stop it, Nathaniel!" I desperately looked around the room.

Had no one seen my struggle? Where was the teacher?

Suddenly the door slammed shut by itself. I began to panic. I was alone with Nathaniel, not a situation I cared to be in.

He twisted my arm behind my back and pulled me in close to him, so our bodies touched. My heart felt as if it was going to explode out of my chest.

"Can you feel it, Harper? Can you feel the electricity soaring through your veins when I touch you? God, the things I want to do to you, the things I can teach you," he purred in my ear. "It will be so much better than your time with William."

Tears escaped my eyes.

"Nathaniel, please, please stop."

"I love it when you beg, Harper, beg for me some more."

"No."

"Funny how your boy William isn't here to rescue you."

I desperately tried to move away from him, but he only pulled me closer. He leant towards me and ran his cool tongue along my neck, stopping at my ear. "If only you would give in to me, things could be so different."

"Stop it. This is so gross. You were with my mother."

"Not in this state I wasn't, so I guess it is totally different," he smirked as he began kissing my ear.

"Give in to me, Harper, let me have you," he whispered seductively in my ear.

Much to my great relief, we were interrupted.

I thought I'd never be happier to see Brittney. "Nathaniel, what is going on in here?"

He let go of my wrist and gently pushed me back.

"Brittney, I didn't hear you come in."

"Clearly," she hissed. "I thought we were going to meet for lunch, Nate?"

"Yeah, babe I'm coming." He said to her then leant in close to me. "This isn't over, Harper. Until tomorrow night?" He picked up my hand and kissed the back of it before walking out of the room with Brittney.

I collapsed against the desk, trying to piece myself back together. I slowed my breathing just as Sid poked her head around the doorframe.

"Harper, lunch?" she called.

"Coming," I called back as I left the room quickly. I dragged my feet to the dining hall.

"Tray?" Sid asked as she held one out to me.

I shook my head. "I'm just going to sit. I'm not really hungry."

Sid leant in close. "You're not pregnant, are you?"

"What? No! What in God's name makes you say that?"

Sid walked over to an empty table and sat down. I sat down opposite her.

"I heard you and Will went to the cabin."

"How? And please don't say news travels fast."

"I have my ways. I'm sure you and Will would have gotten up to no good, God, anyone alone with him would get up to no good." She laughed.

I couldn't control the burning sensation taking over my cheeks.

"Shit, Harper, if I were miles away from this hellhole with one of the most drop-dead-gorgeous boys in school, I'd be getting out the whips and chains if you know what I mean?" Sid raised her eyebrows at me.

I automatically thought of Nathaniel.

"That is disgusting, Sid."

"Well did you two or not?" she asked as she crunched on a carrot stick.

"I don't kiss and tell Sid, sorry."

"Okay then if you won't tell me if you did the dirty deed with William, tell me what's going on with you and Nate?"

"Nate?"

"Yeah, every time you two are in the same room together, the overhead lights start buzzing."

"Shut up," I laughed.

"True?"

"I, there's nothing between us."

"Tell me how then you managed to have both of the hottest guys falling at your feet?"

I looked up and caught Nathaniel watching me from across the room.

"I don't know Sid, I'd rather not talk about it." I looked back down at her tray of half-eaten food.

"Okay." She pushed her tray into the middle of the table and stood up quickly. "I have to go, I'll see you later."

I nodded my head, confused about why she had to leave so abruptly. Suddenly I felt cool fingers run down the back of my neck.

I spun around in my seat to find Nathaniel standing behind me with a grin on his face. I stood up fast.

"You need to leave me alone," I told him firmly.

"Or else?" He held my gaze.

"I think you know what else," I replied angrily as I turned to leave.

He grabbed my wrist. Oh no, not again. I frantically looked around the room; relief swept over me when I realized people were still sitting in their seats.

"I'll scream if you don't let go," I warned him.

"Come back with me to my room, I want to show you something," he said desperately.

"Yeah, no worries Nathaniel, do you really think I'm that stupid?"

"Come on Harper, give in to me, like you did with William," he begged.

I managed to yank my arm free. "You need help Nathaniel, you're sick," I said.

I could feel his eyes burning into my back as I walked away from him, willing myself not to appear frightened by him.

Chapter 30

Back in my room, I closed the door and leant up against it, trying to remain calm. A quick scan of the room revealed a large white box with a red ribbon tied around it on my bed.

I went over to it and picked up the piece of paper that lay folded on top.

Harper,

I want you to wear this to the ball. I chose it for you so that way I know what you are wearing in case I make it out of the infirmary. Be sure to wear the mask at all times and don't take it off.

Raphael has me locked in here like a prisoner. Why, I don't know. I miss you Harper; it is killing me to not be able to see you, touch you. Please be careful tomorrow night.

W. xxx

I wiped away the tears that filled my eyes as I read William's note.

I untied the ribbon and slowly lifted the lid. I drew in a breath, surprised at what I saw lying on top of the white tissue paper – a beautiful black filigree Venetian mask with sparkling red rhinestones and black silk ribbon ties.

Beneath it lay a sexy black satin corset with red ribbon sewn to the boned front and with black lace ribbon ties at the back. It was breathtaking, with its pretty red lace bows also lining the top and bottom edges of the multi-layered ruffle skirt, which was gathered into a tie on one side. I held it against my body and looked in the mirror to see the effect. It was stunning.

I looked back down into the box. A black lace garter belt and thigh-high lace-top fishnet stockings sat folded neatly next to a pair of black-satin closed-toe shoes. The heel was around nine centimetres high and was encrusted with red diamantes, which covered the ankle as well.

How William figured I was going to be able to walk in them was beyond me! I tucked everything neatly back into the box and sat on the edge of the bed thinking about tomorrow night.

A knock at the door interrupted my train of thought. I got up and went to answer it, grateful it was Sid. "Hey Sid, want to come in?"

She looked past me into the room then back to me.

"It's okay Sid, I'm alone."

"Of course you are, no I just came by to tell you there are no lessons tomorrow. Ms Moore wants me to go door knocking to let everyone know. The ball tends to throw everyone into a spin." She looked past me again.

I turned around to see what she was looking at.

"Is that your costume?" she asked.

"Yeah, I'm all set, and you?"

"Oh yeah I can't wait, you know us girls have to be in the ballroom at exactly one minute past seven?" She informed me.

"One minute past seven?" I asked.

"Did you not read the invitation? Anyway, don't leave your room without your mask on."

"Why the mystery?" I questioned her.

She shrugged her shoulders. "I don't know."

"Okay." I smiled at her.

"Well I guess I'll kind of see you at the ball, sort of." She laughed as she turned to leave.

I laughed too. With her fire-red hair it wouldn't matter if she was wearing a mask or not. She was the only one at this school who had hair that colour.

I closed the door and went over to the window and pulled back the heavy drapes. A low mist had rolled in and was covering the lawn. Considering it was the afternoon, it was pretty dark and gloomy.

"I see William sent over your costume?"

I spun around to find Raphael had opened the box and was running his fingers over the corset.

A shiver ran down my back as I watched him. It made me feel uncomfortable the way he was touching it.

"Do you ever knock like a normal person?" I asked.

He looked up and our eyes met.

"Define normal." He smirked as he placed the lid back on the box.

"Forget it. What are you doing in here anyway?"

"I came to tell you that William won't be at the ball tomorrow night; you will be on your own. I can't have him getting in the way."

"What? Why? Nathaniel couldn't have hurt him that bad, I saw the punch he threw."

"It wasn't just the punch, Harper, your little trip to the cabin has taken a lot out of him."

I felt my cheeks turn crimson red; I wasn't sure if it was from embarrassment or anger.

"He asked me to give you this." He reached into his jacket pocket and pulled out a black rectangular box.

I gently took it out of his hands and lifted the lid.

I was taken back at the sheer beauty of the silver dagger lying on the white satin pillow.

I was in awe as I carefully picked it up.

"It is beautiful," I breathed, remembering the first time I laid my eyes on it.

"And very powerful. Only Nephilim offspring can unleash its power, so take care of it. You know how and when to use it, right?" he asked as he made his way over to the door.

"Of course," I nodded.

He smiled at me before walking out of the room and closing the door behind him. I took the box and slipped it under my mattress for safekeeping before I went down to dinner.

That night, I sat by myself in the dining hall. Loud chatter came from every table. Nathaniel was nowhere to be seen, nor was Sid.

I finished up my dinner of macaroni and cheese and strawberry jelly for dessert and headed back to my room. I got changed into my pyjamas and climbed into bed.

I lay awake, staring at the ceiling. My destiny had been set; the dice had been rolled. I forced my eyes closed, hoping sleep wasn't too far away.

Chapter 31

I woke the next morning to heavy rain pelting down on the rooftops of Ella Moore. Thunder roared overhead and lightning was visible through the tops of the drapes.

I glanced over at the clock—a few minutes after eleven in the morning. Really? Had I slept that long?

I got out of bed, went over to the window, opened the curtains and watched the rain streaming down the window. I looked up to the sky, dark storm clouds rolled closer to Ella Moore.

"Great night for the ball," I mumbled, my breath fogging the glass.

"I think it's just perfect."

I turned around to find Sid standing in the doorway.

"Sorry, I knocked but you must have been a million miles away." She smiled.

"No, that's okay, won't you come in?"

She stepped slowly into the room.

"Is there something I can do for you, Sid? You look worried."

She looked over her shoulder into the corridor before closing the door.

"I know what you have to do tonight. If it were me, I wouldn't choose either of them."

I shook my head as I comprehended what she just said.

"Choose?"

"I know you went to the cabin with William, but I still get this feeling he is bad news. Nate too."

"Sid," I stopped her. "You are being silly, you have been warning me since day one about those two, but you have nothing to worry about. William is fine, honestly." I smiled at her.

Sid bit her bottom lip. "Well I have noticed that William has ditched the gothic make-up since he has been hanging around you." She smiled.

"See? Nothing to worry about." I smiled back.

"I know, it's just that I've never had a sister or a best friend that I can look out for, and now I'm being a nervous Nellie."

"I appreciate that. My life has been hell since I arrived here, and I haven't made any friends."

"I'm your friend, but I thought you didn't want to hang around me, so I kept away."

"Are you crazy? I'd love to be your friend, Sid."

"Hey, I have an idea, why don't I come over later and we can get dressed and go to the ball together?"

"I would love that Sid, thank you."

"Okay then, I'll be back here at six thirty; that will give us plenty of time to get ready."

I smiled at Sid as I grabbed my coat and followed her out into the corridor.

I watched as her red hair bobbed its way down the hall.

"Say, Harper?"

I turned to find Brittney, her hips swaying as she made her way over to me. She stopped within inches of my face.

"What is it, Brittney?"

"I've come to tell you to stay away from my boy Nate. He's mine, you can have William," she said, waving her hand generously in the air.

"Oh, I already have." I sneered at her pretty little face.

Her mouth dropped open.

"Why that look, Brit? Haven't you and Nate ever? Oh I'm sorry, that might just be my fault, he can't seem to keep away from me or his hands off me either. He's using you as a distraction, sad really."

Before she could say anything, I turned on my heels and headed off down the corridor. It felt so good to stand up to her.

I decided a walk in the rain would give me some time to think. Low mist made the grounds look eerie, although I could still make out a couple in the gazebo holding each other and stealing a kiss every now and then. I thought of William and my heart ached. I couldn't believe I had to face this night without him. It didn't seem fair. I passed the kissing couple and headed further into the grounds. I had never seen such a beautiful forest. Peering into the mist, I could just make out a hidden garden.

I walked down two stone steps that led into a circular garden planted with beaded topiary, soft pink camellias, purple hydrangeas and roses, whose vibrant colours were amazing. In the midst of all this beauty, in the centre of the garden stood a gurgling fountain and cobblestone paths wound their way between trimmed box hedges. Two stone benches with angel heads on the ends of the armrests sat opposite each other. It was a magnificent sight.

"Wow!" I said, as I admired my surroundings.

"Beautiful, isn't it?"

I spun around to find Nathaniel standing at the top of the steps. He was dressed completely in black, holding a long-stemmed red rose in his hand.

His hair was wet and tousled, and his eyes were sparkling. My heart skipped a beat. He slowly came down the steps and headed over to me, stopping close to me. I looked up into his eyes.

"Hi." He smiled.

"Hi." I blushed. "What are you doing here?" It felt like my heart was tightening up.

"I wanted to be alone with you to say I'm sorry, so I followed you here. I'm trying, Harper; I don't want to be bad anymore. Can you help me?"

I saw the pain in his eyes; I reached up and brushed back his hair, which had fallen across his face.

"I'm sorry, Nathaniel, but you and I can never happen."

"I wasn't myself when I was with your mother, you have to believe me," he pleaded.

"I'm sorry, but the thought just grosses me out."

He dropped the rose to the ground, its dark red petals turning black. He took my face in his hands. "We kissed, Harper, before you knew anything about me. Don't tell me you didn't want me then."

"Nathaniel I was lost, confused, I had just arrived here, my best friend was dead and the two most beautiful boys in school were fighting for my attention, little did I know why. I'm sorry if I led you to think any differently. I'm with William now, I have given myself to him, I'm sorry."

His hands fell to his sides, and he hung his head. He stood for a while, not saying anything.

I decided to break the awful silence. "I have to go."

As I stepped around him, he grabbed my wrist. I suddenly became very frightened.

"Nathaniel?"

"One dance, that's all I ask," he said as he let go of my wrist.

My mind flashed to the dagger lying in the black box under my mattress.

"Give me one dance," he said.

I looked into his eyes; they were full of so much hurt and pain.

"I swear I will never talk to you again. I will leave you alone. I don't want to hurt you anymore. I'm in love with you, Harper, let me love you," he begged.

"I can't Nathaniel, I'm sorry. You are what you are. Nothing will change that."

"And William? What about what he is?"

I shivered at the thought of William and me in bed together.

"It's different, he's not like you."

"Not like me?" He chuckled.

I didn't like the look in his eyes. They had turned dark and menacing.

"I have to go," I told him.

"Why are you so afraid of me?" he asked through clenched teeth.

I looked up into his eyes. Was he for real? Fear enveloped me as he took a step closer.

"You've tried to kill me Nathaniel, more than once. You killed my best friend, you slept with my mother, which technically makes you my father, which in turn makes me sick to the stomach even trying to process that thought. You hurt William to the point he is in the hospital, do I need to go on?" I spat.

"I'm not a monster, Harper."

"You're not a monster?" I scoffed. "You are trying to kill me, Nathaniel, what does that make you then, besides dark, twisted, totally inhuman? A monster?"

He shook his head and gave me a dark smile. "No, Harper," he reached for my hands and held them loosely in his. "Not anymore. I've realized I don't want to hurt you. I want to love you and for you to love me. Please believe me."

I pulled my hands out of his. "I'm sorry, Nathaniel, but you and I are never going to happen."

I turned to leave and didn't look back as I headed up the steps and away from him.

The garden didn't seem so beautiful anymore.

Chapter 32

Six thirty came around all too quickly, and Sid was knocking at the door.

"It's open," I called as I laid out my outfit on the bed.

"Well, look at your sexy costume," she exclaimed as she came in closing the door behind her.

"A little too sexy for me," I replied.

We got dressed in our corsets, layered skirts, fishnet stockings and high-heeled shoes.

"This is going to be the best ball yet!" Sid exclaimed, placing a blue headband with a feather attached to it on her head.

I looked at her and laughed. She was like a small child in a candy store.

"You're super-excited, aren't you?" I asked her.

"Aren't you? This is like what we all look forward to here," she replied as she tied her mask on her face.

"Yeah I am," I lied.

Sid helped me pin up half my hair and tie up my mask.

"I feel silly dressed like this." I tugged on the raised part of my skirt. There was too much leg showing. Sid slapped my hand away.

"When you've got it love, and believe me you have, flaunt it. You look amazing, Harper, I don't know if the boys are going to be able to stay away from you tonight."

I gave her an uneasy smile as she headed out the door.

"Oh, wait, I need to make sure the window is closed, I opened it earlier to let some fresh air in," I said to Sid as I turned back into my room.

I checked over my shoulder to make sure Sid wasn't following me. I grabbed the dagger and placed it through my garter belt, under my skirt.

"All set?" She looked at me suspiciously as I came back out.

"Yeah, I must have already closed it." I smiled.

She nodded her head, not entirely convinced I was telling the truth.

We made it to the ballroom at exactly one minute past seven. Cancan dancers and courtesans were sitting at round tables that were covered in red tablecloths with little candles in the centre.

It took me a few minutes to get used to the dim room. The only light came from the candles.

"The boys will be here any minute now, so this is where I leave you. Have fun!"

Before I could answer her or even register her odd departure, she danced her way across the room. I looked around at all the masked faces and suddenly the girls who had been sitting were now standing and all looking expectantly towards the double doors. You could feel the excitement in the air.

The music turned up and as the doors opened. I never realized how many boys were actually at this school.

They made their way into the room towards the girls to ask them to dance.

"May I?"

I turned to find a boy holding out his hand to me. I looked up into his masked eyes. Brown. Not Nathaniel or William.

"Sure." I smiled as he took my hand in his.

He led me to the dance floor and pulled me close; a little too close.

"You smell like vanilla," he said, sniffing my neck.

I pulled back a little. "Yes." I smiled as he twirled me around.

I wondered if William was here, if Raphael had let him out of the hospital.

"Your mind seems to be somewhere else," the boy said.

"I'm sorry, yes, it is. Would you excuse me?"

I let go of his hand and walked over to the drinks table. My feet were already hurting, and I wanted nothing more than to take off the corset.

"I like your costume," a voice whispered ever so softly in my ear.

I began to turn around.

"No, don't turn around," he said as he ran his hand up my thigh.

I grabbed his wrist, pushed it away and turned around.

Brown eyes.

"How dare you," I spat.

"How about you and I dance?" he asked.

"Hell would have to freeze over first!" I pushed past him and found Sid sitting at a table with a boy dressed in a red tailcoat jacket, black trousers and a black mask.

"I need to talk to you," I interrupted them.

"Now's not the right time," she said through tight lips.

"The boy turned around to look at me. I couldn't see the colour of his eyes.

"Please, it's important," I begged.

She looked down at her watch. "Meet me in the courtyard in five, okay?"

I could tell she was angry with me. The boy hadn't taken his eyes off me.

"Don't worry, it's okay, sorry I bothered you," I said sadly.

I walked away, feeling lost and so uncomfortable in my outfit. The night seemed to drag on.

Around nine, I decided to head out to the balcony and was surprised to find I was alone. The rain had eased but the mist was still around. I closed my eyes and inhaled deeply, taking in the smell of wet lawn.

I suddenly felt someone close behind me and opened my eyes. He ran his hands down my arms and stopped at my hands, entwining his fingers through mine.

He leant in close and ran his nose up my neck. I couldn't move; he had me pinned.

"You smell nice and you look divine."

I tried to turn around, but he pushed his body closer to mine. "I want you to come find me just before midnight," he whispered in my ear before letting go of my hands.

I turned around just in time to catch his red tailcoat head back inside and get lost in the crowd. It was the boy who had been sitting with Sid.

Chapter 33

The closer the clock ticked to midnight, the more anxious I became.

I walked around aimlessly amongst tuxedos, masks and corsets, refusing to dance with anyone that asked me. I was lost in a sea of colour, laughter and dancing. I just wanted this night to be over.

"It's almost midnight," a girl called over her shoulder to another girl who was following close behind her.

"I can't wait," the other girl replied as they rushed past me.

Midnight, now there was a word I wished didn't exist. I had no luck in finding William, it was clear he was a no-show, and as for Nathaniel, I was at a loss.

I felt a hand around my wrist. "Dance with me," the voice said, as he led me onto the dance floor.

I looked up into his masked face; he was too tall to be Nate or William. He pulled me close to him. "You know what you have to do, Harper, time is running out."

I leant forward to get a better look at his face. "Raphael?" I whispered.

He nodded his head. "You need to find Nate soon."

"You expect me to do it here, in front of all these people?" I spoke softly.

"Take him to the gazebo, no one will be outside."

"So you want me to flirt with him, lead him on and then kill him?"

"Do what you have to do to get him outside."

I saw Raphael look behind me. "It's him, he is coming," he whispered, making me shiver.

I froze, unable to move.

"May I please have this dance?" Nathaniel asked.

Raphael kissed the back of my hand before he bowed and left us standing there, face to face.

I looked over his red tailcoat and black mask. "I hope I have chosen right," he began.

"Are you looking for someone in particular?" I asked.

"I'm not allowed to say names."

"You are the one who was outside with me?" I cut him off.

"Yes, I have been watching you all night, there is something intriguing about you." He smiled.

"I need some fresh air, care to walk with me outside?" I flirted.

Nathaniel reached for my hand as we walked through the crowd.

"You know we are meant to be inside dancing?" he remarked as we reached the bottom step outside.

"I know, but it's so crowded in there." I walked him over to the gazebo.

Raphael was right; nobody had come outside. Still holding his hand, I led him into the gazebo. You could hear the music softly spilling outside.

I pulled Nathaniel into a slow dance and began swaying to the music.

"Who are you?" he asked softly.

I looked into his mask-covered eyes.

"You'll find out soon enough," I said as I ran my hand down the side of his face.

My stomach was churning having to pretend like this.

He pulled me in close to him. "I have to do something," he said as we swayed to the music. "But I don't want to. Come with me to the willow tree."

I pulled back and looked at him. "What?"

"I don't know who you are, and you don't know me. I need someone to talk to, we are too close to Ella Moore here."

He was right. We were too close.

I swallowed. "Okay."

He took my hand in his and led me out of the gazebo, across the lawn and over to the willow tree.

We stood, facing each other, not speaking a word.

Nathaniel walked a full circle around me; he looked so mysterious in his mask. He then went and stood behind me. Fear washed over me; did he know who I was? He took a step closer, placed his hands on my hips and gently pulled me back towards him.

I felt his lips brush my ear as he spoke. "I need to do something, something very bad to someone I am very much in love with. It's not right, I shouldn't be feeling this way, it's just not me."

I slowly turned around to face him and looked into his eyes.

"Who is she, this girl you are talking about?" I asked, already knowing what his answer was going to be.

I just wanted to hear it from him.

Nate reached up and before I had time to realize what he was doing, he untied my mask with one hand and gently pulled it away from my face.

"You," he whispered as he pushed me hard against the tree trunk, letting my mask fall to the grass. He took off his mask and threw it to the ground next to mine.

"Do you know how much it is killing me that you don't want me like I want you?" he asked as he closed the gap between us.

"But how...?"

"Did I know?" he finished my sentence.

I nodded.

"As if I wouldn't know, Harper. Who do you think sent you that alluring outfit?" Nathaniel ran his cool fingers across my bare chest.

"But I thought..."

He shook his head as an evil smile crossed his lips.

"You know William will be looking for me?" I lied.

"William?" He chuckled as his hand made its way up my neck.

I tried frantically to pull it away as his grip tightened.

"William, William, William! Do you not know how much I crave you? It is consuming me more than ever," he snarled.

I could feel my feet lifting off the ground.

"Nathaniel, please stop!" I choked as he lifted me higher.

"It's always William, you wanted me too once, Harper!" he cried.

"I know, I know. I do want you, Nathaniel, please, please let me down," I lied as a tear rolled down my flushed cheek.

Slowly he brought me back down to the ground.

"You want me?" he asked, not quite believing me.

I felt the ground beneath my feet as he loosened his grip on my neck.

"I couldn't decide, Nathaniel. I think I made the wrong choice sleeping with William," I said quickly as I took a step closer to him. "You were right, I should have chosen you, I'm sorry," I said as I gently kissed his lips.

He pulled back, and then fell to his knees, burying his face in his hands.

"I'm sorry, Harper," he mumbled not looking up.

I stood there watching him as he fell apart before me.

Run Harper, run back closer to Ella Moore. William's voice screamed in my head.

Without a second thought I turned as ran as fast as I could in high heels back towards Ella Moore.

Chapter 34

As the dark night surrounded me, I ran faster. I heard the clock tower chime, eleven forty-five. Time was running out.

I kicked off my shoes and took a sharp right towards the back of Ella Moore, avoiding the direct path to the terrace. Going inside would be pointless; I still had a job to do.

To my horror, Nathaniel jumped out at me from behind a large tree. I came to an abrupt stop.

"Harper, Harper, Harper," he shook his head. "Did you really think you could outrun me?"

I was out of breath and a sharp pain was making its way up my side.

"What do you want from me?" I screamed at him breathlessly.

He moved in close and ran his hand down the side of my face, stopping at my neck.

"I already told you, it's you I want." He said as he tightened his grip on my neck once again.

Suddenly, he lifted me up and we were soaring high up into the night sky.

His wings were black as a raven's and appeared as if they stretched out for miles.

I couldn't breathe. I tried to scream but no sound came from my lips.

"You lied to me, it's William you want, not me!" he howled, almost sounding animalistic.

I tried to pry his hand away from my neck but failed. We were heading down now.

"Where's William now, huh?" he shouted angrily, as he placed his other hand on my chest.

Without warning, he took his hand from my neck, pushing me downwards with great force.

I was flying backwards, and then suddenly I felt my back hit something hard. A smashing sound filled the quiet night. As I fell in a heap on the grass, tiny shards of coloured glass rained down on me from above like a broken rainbow.

He had thrown me against the angel stained-glassed window that I saw in the old library. I could feel thick blood trickling down my forehead and over my left eye.

Was it over? Had Nathaniel won? I couldn't find the strength to get up.

He came and knelt down in front of me and placed his fingers under my chin. He raised my face to his.

"If I can't have you, neither can William," he said, wrapping his hand around my throat again. He picked me up off the ground by my neck and once again we were flying up through the night sky, heading for the rooftops of Ella Moore.

I tried to shake myself free from his hold, but I barely had the strength to struggle. As I stared at Nathaniel, his face was going in and out of focus and I felt like I was going to pass out.

Kicking my legs frantically and tugging at his hand around my neck, I reached down with my free hand and grabbed the dagger from underneath my skirt.

In one swift move, using the last bit of strength I had, I plunged the dagger into his chest—just as the clock chimed midnight.

"I'm finished with you, Nathaniel!" I screamed at the top of my voice, as thunder roared overhead.

"What have you done?" he gasped.

His eyes turned black as ebony, and the veins in his neck fluorescent blue. He looked terribly frightening.

If he let go of my neck, I was sure to fall to my death.

"I will take you with me," he hissed.

"NEVER!" I yelled at the top of my lungs as I pushed the dagger deeper into his chest.

We froze in mid-air. As he withered uncontrollably, his grip on my neck was still tight. Then as he took, he last breath he let me go.

I began to fall, watching in disbelief as Nathaniel began to evaporate in a cloud of grey mist. I closed my eyes, waiting to hit the ground—and then surely death would follow.

Nothing happened. The wind stopped rushing around me, and it felt like I was going up rather than down, quite gracefully I might add. I wasn't sure what was going on. Then I started floating downwards. Was I dead? Was this my descent to Heaven? I slowly opened my eyes to a blinding white light and wings; beautiful, big white wings that stretched out forever and which enfolded my body.

"William," I exhaled in relief.

"I'm here now, it's over," he rasped as he slowly lowered me to the ground, cradling me against his naked torso in his strong arms.

"It's over?" I asked as I closed my eyes briefly, then opened them again.

I felt an eerie calmness wash over me; William's eyes never left mine.

"Yes," he said softly with a half-smile on his lips. "Do you believe in angels now?" he teased.

"Yes," I murmured, as I gazed upon his beautiful white angel wings and the white light that surrounded us.

William opened his arms and slipped me gently onto the cool grass beside him. I watched in disbelief as his wings slowly disappeared from his body and the gleaming white light also vanished, leaving only the soft glow of the moonlight illuminating us.

William hung his head and let out a couple of deep breaths. He looked weary.

"William, are you okay?" I whispered.

He raised his tired eyes to mine. "Am I okay?" he asked. "What about you?" He gently took my chin in his hand and moved my face to get a better look at my neck. "He hurt you pretty bad."

I lowered my eyes. "I'm fine."

"You think? By the look of those marks around your neck," he paused and shook his head, "he almost had you, Harper."

"I had it under control, William," I lied as I looked back up into his eyes.

William shook his head. "It took every last bit of my powers to stop you from falling to your death."

I shivered at his words. "I know… you saved me from hitting the ground."

William pulled me into his arms and held me tight. I breathed in his scent before I pulled back and looked at him.

My mind began racing in every direction. Was he mortal now?

"Does this mean it's over for you?" I whispered fearfully.

"No, Harper, it's not over," he replied tenderly. "This is just the beginning…"

I rested my head against his chest and smiled, certain I could hear the beat of his mortal heart.

About the Author

Jo Donato is a wife and mother of two; she is based in Adelaide, South Australia. When she is not hiding in her writing room talking to her characters with her trusty blue roan Cocker Spaniel sidekick, Arlo, by her side and her Cocker Spaniel, Daisy, in her heart, you can find her getting lost in a book or baking in the kitchen.

Crossfire is her debut novel.

You can follow her author page on Instagram @jodonatoauthor

www.ingramcontent.com/pod-product-compliance
Lightning Source LLC
Chambersburg PA
CBHW060642260626
47161CB00008B/2967